The Honeyspike

A NOTE ON THE AUTHOR

Bryan MacMahon is one of Ireland's most distinguished writers. He has written novels, plays, ballads and collections of short stories. His historical pageant *A Pageant of Ireland* ran for sixteen years in a medieval castle in Clare and was seen by over half a million people. He lives in Listowel, County Kerry.

The Honeyspike

BRYAN MACMAHON

POOLBEG

First published in 1967 by
The Bodley Head Ltd
Paperback edition 1993 by
Poolbeg Press Ltd,
Knocksedan House,
123 Baldoyle Industrial Estate,
Dublin 13, Ireland

This edition published in 1995

© Bryan MacMahon 1967

The moral right of the author has been asserted.

A catalogue record for this book is available from the British Library.

ISBN 1 85371 310 4

Cover photograph by Mike O'Toole
Cover design by Poolbeg Group Services Ltd
Printed by The Guernsey Press Ltd,
Vale, Guernsey, Channel Islands.

Also by Bryan MacMahon
and published by Poolbeg

The Master
Memoirs of a Listowel Schoolmaster

TO MY SONS
AND JOAN

ONE

Here is a tale of the Irish roads, of a tinker
  and his wife.
It's a tale of trouble and wildness and a child
  that's born to life.
There's mating in it, birth and death, and drink
  to flood a dyke;
So here's how they raced the coloured road
  that led to the Honey Spike.

It starts with harness ringing by the Causeway
  of the North.
It ends with an infant crying in the mountains
  of the South.
There's mating in it, birth and death, and drink
  to flood a dyke;
So here's how they raced the bloody road
  that led to the Honey Spike.

(1)

The island lay about three miles from the Antrim shore. Its cliffs were white, almost silver. The water of the sound was angry with whitecaps, and the sky above it alive with the glitter of gulls' wings.

Northeast of the island, the Paps of Jura were pencilled on the horizon: to the northwest the sea gave the impression of stretching away until it met the icecap at the North Pole.

On the mainland, the road was raised high above the sea. Below the road, the cliffside fell sharply down to the hexagonal pillars of the Giants' Causeway.

Walking eastward in light fur-lined boots, the tinker girl came round a bend of the road. She carried a basket on her arm. Her red and green tartan shawl was thrown back from her head and encircled her back like a sash.

The girl's tanned face was lean. Her eyes were blue, and her weather-bleached hair was drawn back from her forehead. The girl wore hair slides, earrings, and bangles.

As she walked, her head seemed tilted to an angle of tension.

Motorcars raced past her, but she did not alter her gait. Once she looked out at the island and the mountains; then she shifted her gaze to the northwest.

Presently she heard the faint noise of harness bells approaching from the west.

Her face set in hardness as the jig of the hooves of an unshod pony and the race of light wheels drew nearer. Reaching a point where, in a lay-by, the fence on the seaward side of the road had given place to a timber railing with a wicket gate set in it, the girl came to a halt. Behind the wicket was a black notice board bearing a legend in white.

The girl drew off the highway and set her basket on the ground. Her face was now sulky. As she opened her shawl to draw it fully about her, she was seen to be heavily pregnant. Half screened by a fuchsia bush, she rested her forearms on the railing and looked down the cliffside to the Causeway below. A few tourists clambered over the rocks.

A tinker's flat cart, drawn by a piebald cob, drew nearer.

Reins in hand, a young tinker man stood upright in the body of the cart. As he passed the place where the girl was standing, the driver suddenly saw her and pulled sharply on the reins. He kept his balance as the animal came to a halt.

The young man swung the cob completely around on the roadway and pulled into the lay-by to the east of where the girl was standing. He leaped lightly out of the cart and, moving to the animal's head, knotted the rope reins about the base of a fuchsia bush.

All the while his dark brown eyes hung on the girl, who, since his arrival, had not altered her position. The man went back to the cart, pushed aside a dozen newly made tin measures and some rods and canvas, and tugged out an armful of hay. This he dropped at the cob's head.

"There, Tomboy!" he said.

His eyes alive over the red-brown stubble of beard, the man continued to watch the woman. As he adjusted the knot on the yellow scarf at his throat, his lower jaw began to jut a little. With a flick of his thumbnail, he raised his hatbrim off his forehead. The morning sunlight lighted up his face.

He thrust his hands deep into the bias-cut pockets in the front of his out-of-fashion breeches so that the folds of his cutaway check coat were bunched behind him. With slow movements of exaggerated maleness, he walked towards the girl.

About a yard from her he halted and glanced down into the basket.

"Did you do good?" he asked.

"I done bad!"

The tinker man turned his back on the sea, and, easing his elbow points on to the railing, viewed the rough land that lay to the other side of the road. He looked up at the sky.

As if savouring a secret pleasure, the while his hat hung balanced on his poll, he turned to look out at the island and the sea. His eyes roamed the horizon from east to west. He smiled in satisfaction.

A stray coil of the girl's hair was moved by the breeze.

The man turned and again looked down into the basket: it contained a variety of objects—tiepins and studs, camphor balls, hair slides, small reproductions of the Sacred Heart mounted on ovals of red baize, printed "Home Blessings," a swatch of broadsheet ballads printed in a variety of colours, and odds and ends of country finery.

"You sold nothin' at all?" he said.

"I told you I done bad!'

"I done bad, too! Twelve cans goin' out, a dozen comin' back. The North's a hungry country."

The girl continued to glare at the scene below her.

"If this is the part of Ireland that has been stolen from

us," the man went on, "as far as Martin Claffey is concerned the country can stay divided till the crack o' hell."

The girl made no response. Martin drew his hands quickly out of his pockets and said, "Breda, I crossed that bridge!"

"What bridge?"

"The one I was tellin' you of in the camp last night."

The girl gave a noncommittal exclamation.

"A lump of rocky island there beyond," Martin went on. "The cliff top here. One footplank with guide ropes for the hands, stretching out across this gully between shore an' rock. Forty paces to this little bridge. The sea foamin' below."

Listlessly, "You crossed it?"

"At first it cowarded me. Then: 'Blast you for a bridge,' says I. I seen the fishermen outside at the rock's foot, laughin' up at me. As I was standin' there, down the cliffside comes a lad of ten or so with a fisherman's dinner under his arm. An', without settin' a finger on either rope, he skips across the swingin' plank. 'You be damned!' says I, an' I talkin' to the bridge. Out I goes! Midways I stopped. When I looked down I almost sweated my blood. Then I said that no Antrim bridge'd coward a Southern travellin' man. An', begod, I crossed. I threw myself sweatin' on the rocks at the other side." After a pause: "If goin' out was bad, Breda, comin' back was worse. But I done it, just the same!"

Martin Claffey strutted away from his wife. Looking up at the notice board, his face darkened.

"What does the board say?" he asked.

"The Giants' Causeway."

Martin half opened the wicket gate and looked down

14

along the pathway that led from the cliffside to the shore below. He saw the basalt formation piled at the sea edges with the breakers foaming around its tip.

"The Giants' Causeway! We're at the very top of Ireland, so?"

"Aye!"

"We're a long road from Kerry now."

"We are, indeed!" There was something of scorn to her tone.

"Can we go no further to the North?"

"Aye, if you care to walk the water.'

Martin laughed. "When you go back to Kerry in the South, you'll have somethin' to boast about."

"What's that?"

"That you travelled the length of Ireland in your husband's cart."

Breda's eyes narrowed.

"What you've seen in a year!" Martin went on. " 'Twas after Puck Fair in Kerry this time twelvemonths that we were married, wasn't it?"

The girl did not reply.

"We had a flamin' weddin', you an' me. We tied the Claffeys an' the Gilligans together, so that as one they can face any tribe in Ireland."

"Even the Buck McQueens?"

Silence fell between them. The girl turned over her left hand and glared into the palm of it.

"You're always lookin' into your old hand," he said.

"What if I am?"

"What does it do for you?"

"It helps me to think back."

"What do you see in it now?"

"I see sky an' sea, starvation an' good feedin'. I see drink an' drought, Christmas an' Easter, love an' hate, life an' death. I even see farmers an' priests, cats an' fish."

"Are you jokin'?"

"Maybe I am an' maybe I amn't," Breda said. "How could I tell?"

(2)

As a child, Breda Gilligan had known young Claffey by eyesight for many years.

She had marked him out from the swarm of other dirty-faced brats on the roads. She had noted his head of copper-coloured hair, his mutinous eyes, his devil-be-damned stand and strut.

Yet she had never spoken to him. Young as she was, she was aware that the relationship of a tribe to tinkers outside their *cut,* or traditional area of travel, was one of hostility.

She recalled having seen him first at Cahirmee Horse Fair.

He was then a boy dressed in overlong breeches with two front pockets into which his grubby hands were dug deep. Even then he wore the long coat, the yellow kerchief, with the jaunty hat drawn firmly over his eyes.

Horses cluttered up the broad street of the fair, hunters with good blood in their movements, Irish draught horses and Connemara ponies. Breda liked the smell of fresh horse dung: to some extent it conveyed the essence of her wandering life.

At Cahirmee, then! From where she stood against a whitewashed wall, she watched young Claffey move up to the hindquarters of a piebald stallion pony; the pony was dancing restlessly as a knot of yelling tinkers tried to browbeat the old farmer-owner into selling the animal at a price far below his market value.

The shouting group of wranglers kept away from the hindquarters of the stallion—all except young Claffey: flicking his hatbrim upwards, the youngster strode up to the rear of the stallion and slapped it on the rump.

The startled stallion showed two crescents of bloodshot eyes. Hissing defiance and moving directly behind the hooves, Martin combed the tangled tail with his crooked fingers; when the hair was freed he tied it into a simple knot, which he drew tight with a jerk that sent the stallion rearing forward.

With a final hiss of defiance, Martin had thrust his hands into his pockets and strutted away.

Breda's eyes had followed Claffey.

Where had she seen him for the second time? She groped back to the Whitsun "Patteran" of Ballyvourney.

She had begged a Japanese chip bird from a stall-holder. The bird had a broken yellow tail, yellow wings, and a blue body; spun at the end of a stick, it whirled and whistled erratically. She was eleven years of age at the time: seated on a low wall in mid-village she twirled the bird in figures-of-eight.

Among the crowds of country people paying the "rounds" at the holy well moved gangs of tinkers from different parts of Munster.

For Breda Gilligan, barefooted, her belly full of victuals from her uncle's skillet, the sun shining, the blue bird circling, the crowds streaming forward, the prayers of the country folk calling on Saint Gobnait for aid, all added up to a wild natural contentment.

The warmth of the sunny wall penetrating her buttocks, she continued to twirl the bird. She was suddenly aware of a pair of brown eyes watching the bird.

Claffey had grown. He now appeared to be about thirteen years of age. Although he was older than she, Breda knew that, in the awareness of the world of men and women gained from the recurrent avoidance of randy hands, she could cancel the two years between them. She also knew that, as long as the bird kept circling, the boy would remain watching.

Between the Claffeys and her own Gilligans there was a vague air of watchfulness. Nothing like what lay between her clan and the Buck McQueens—that was blood. But suspicion there certainly was—suspicion of the half-understood travellers like the Claffeys who sometimes crossed the Shannon into Clare and ventured even into the remote territories called Galway or Sligo.

Breda's nose crinkled as she noted the phlegm-track shining below the boy's nostrils. Yet, she thought, water and soap would work wonders with him. Why did she want to keep Claffey there? she asked herself.

She kept twisting the bird round and round. The yellow tail moved well, if brokenly, in the sunlight.

Out of an eye corner she watched his mother, Poll-Poll Claffey, at the wellside. A country woman with a mother-o'-pearl rosary in her hands scowled at the whining tinker.

Breda's eye returned to the boy. Stay there, fool! she kept saying without speaking. "Watch the bird," she said softly. Then, surprising even herself, she added, "Later you will watch me."

Martin Claffey's mouth had fallen open. Breda had the impression of watching one who was asleep.

The old lady with the rosary had begun to abuse Poll-

Poll Claffey. "Tinkers cluttering up the blessed pool!" she said in a loud voice

Poll-Poll's face was dull with an anger she thought it wiser to conceal. What was this bloody craw-thumper screechin' about? Hadn't she herself inherited from her mother and grandmother the right to sell "blessed" water at sixpence a glass? Was she goin' to give it up now because of the caterwaulin' of this hen? No one liked to have a scene on the holiday—this Poll-Poll knew and traded on to the full. In answer to the tight-lipped attack she had begun to wheedle: "Wisha, God love you, missus. We must all live!"

Mingling complaint with prayer, the bitter pilgrim moved on.

"Give us th' ould bird!"

The abrupt request startled Breda. Martin Claffey's right hand had come out of his pocket, and his grubby forefinger was pointing at the whirling wings.

The quicker movement of the bird's flight indicated her scorn.

"You'd swear 'twas real," Martin said, "the way your eyes are watchin' it." His features had gathered angrily together.

The bird clatter-whistled in defiance.

"Gi'e us wan swing outa it?"

"I won't!" She added, contemptuously, "Claffey!" The boy's face became congested. His left hand came out of his fob pocket; both hands became soiled fists.

He glared from the bird to the girl and back again. His eyes turned to look at his mother, then moved sharply backwards towards the tents and stalls. His eyes flickered over chalk Infants of Prague, chalk cocks, and silver coins set on black shawls.

His gaze returned to the girl and the bird. He shifted his stance from one leg to the other. In his eyes anger was replaced by craft.

"I'll give you a napple if you give me a swing."

He took a bitten apple out of his pocket, rubbed the scarlet skin of the fruit on the seat of his breeches until it glowed. The bitten part was the colour of rust. He offered the fruit to the girl from a grubby palm.

She sniffed her refusal.

" 'Tis sweet," he said, taking a bite out of the fruit.

The bird went on twirling.

After several angry bites, "I've a good bloody mind to take it off you!" he said, throwing the core away.

Still Breda did not speak.

She found herself in a whirl of controlled excitement. She looked out through the circle made by the spinning bird at the two fists clenching and unclenching against the tattered breeches.

Stalemate. By implication, it spelled victory for the girl.

In silence she pleaded with the bird: Bird, continue to entice. Together we will get what we seek—the explosion of violence.

One of Martin's patched boots had taken a step towards her. Breda was conscious of a pleasurable churning in her throat.

"Hey, Claffey!"

Martin and Breda glanced up. Breda's face clouded.

In the first womanhood of eighteen, Winifred McQueen, a gypsy square of cloth on her head, a new shawl wrapping her round, was eyeing the pair.

"Claffey," the newcomer said scornfully, "come on wi' me an' don't be playin' wi' childer."

Her head thrown back, her eyes glinting, Winifred strode away.

For a moment, Martin stood irresolute. As Breda began to make the bird spin violently, the cord broke and the bird leaped through the air to fall at his feet.

Martin raised his boot and ground it down on the toy. The bird crackled as it was crunched into the clay. Martin raced after Winifred McQueen.

Breda struggled off the wall. "You'll pay for that, you bastar'!" she screamed.

From the wellside, Poll-Poll looked up in amusement.

The pious spinster made the sign of the Cross on herself. "The scum of Ireland are soiling the fields of the Lord," she breathed.

(3)

The old Jesuit, Father Melody, walked along the pathway by the side of the ornamental lake in St. Stephen's Green, Dublin.

"To hell with the Jesuits!" he chortled to himself.

Having said this three times, he raised his face to the sky and added . . . "is the cry that rings through Europe today."

Father Melody laughed.

Wasn't that a lunatic text for a famous Jesuit preacher to take for his sermon? "That shook 'em!" he chuckled and then, inconsequentially, began chanting in an undertone: "*Non omnis moriar: multaque pars mei vitabit Libitinam.*"

He stopped and looked down at the flower beds.

"*Pel . . . Pelar . . . Pelargonium . . .* the Latin name

for a plant approximating to the common geranium often escapes my tongue," he told himself. I must look awkward with this ungainly lope of mine, he thought. Then: Too late now to make a change.

"Heigh-ho, and a blinkin' bottle of rum," Father Melody hummed as he moved on.

He felt tempted to skip: his years and his thick-soled boots were against the notion. He crossed the ornamental bridge in mid-park and trudged down the asphalt walk, past the rows of students sprawling in deck chairs, male alternating with female, their notebooks indolently before and beside them.

"De Sexto," the priest muttered, "always it will be *De Sexto.* Good bloody job there *is* original sin in the world; otherwise all of us—Jays, Doms, Vins, Caps, Reds, Obbles, Frans, and Passionate Fathers—would be at the Labour Exchange signing on for the do-dee-O-dole."

"Ah'm a poor Jesuit," Father Melody told himself, in nigger-minstrel mimicry. "Ah'm canting, hypocritical, Jesuitical, Tartuffish, Machiavellian, Janus-faced, forsworn and perfidious. Me—Melody. Or am I?"

The priest hummed happily; he ceased humming as he remembered the confrontation in the Rector's study.

"Yes, Father Rector?" "Ah, Father Jim—there you are. Sit down . . . take those papers—yes, leave them anywhere."

The rectorial glare now beats on the frayed cuffs, the dandruff on the collar and lapels, the boots that make a din on convent corridors. "How did you like the Spa at Lisdoonvarna? Smells like bad eggs, the sulphur water, eh?"

The mingled laughter.

"Father Jim, what's this I wished to see you about? Oh,

22

yes, it's this proposed Metropolitan Committee on Itinerants."

Ah, Father Melody told himself, then Ah again. No matter how mad, abstruse, daft, insignificant, or droll your interest, the Jays had it pigeonholed under the head of Talents—Various.

So that, on an occasion like this, an authority was forthcoming.

"It's becoming quite a problem . . . ," the Rector said.

"Who? What?"

"The itinerants . . . can't open a newspaper without . . . By the by, I've nominated you to represent us on the Committee. I've got the approval of . . . you know. . . . All, of course, subject to your willingness to act."

The itinerants! Hah! Be the hokey fiddle, I like that. Bedam, I do. But I must not pretend to be eager.

Over bifocals, the Rector: "You *are* willing to act, of course?"

(Nod, you clerical rascal, nod. Clear your throat and speak up.)

"Yes, Father Rector."

"Good."

"Who else is on this Committee? Is there a chap by the name of Gleeson?"

"I don't think so. Gleeson?"

"A pity. He knows more about the problem than the rest of us."

"Is he the fellow who wrote that piece in *The Tongue?* Brilliant in patches. But unstable. He's not on it. Can't be helped now."

"The danger is . . ."

"Danger?"

" . . . that the Committee will turn out to be a crowd

23

of professional do-gooders who—excuse the expression, Father Rector—will achieve sweet damn-all. People who'll recite the rosary once a year in front of a caravan and enter it on twenty forms. And holy women who'll wipe the sn— excuse the expression, Father Rector—the mucus from the nose of a tinker kid, say: 'Repeat *a, b, c, d,* child,' and 'Suffer little children . . .' and then see that the local reporter hears all about it."

"We'll never evolve a perfect society, Father."

"We'll evolve grades of it if we have savvy."

"All I do hope is that you don't get impatient."

(He meant "eccentric," Father Melody told himself.)

"Won't promise anything," he said aloud. Never promise anything. Daresay prominent craw-thumpers will be co-opted later, he thought. Oh, Divine Lord! And the authorities. And the teaching profession. And the Children of God. And the Knights of St. Ridiculus Mus. And the League of Grateful Clients. Holy Mother the Church— that's me. Aloud: "Father Rector, is an itinerant on it?"

The Rector laughed a tolerant, amused "N-o-o-o!"

"Not even one hairy, verminous, porter-saturated ould tinker?"

Again the laugh, hinting at the end of patience and tolerance.

"Are they to be tried and convicted without the slightest attempt at hearing evidence on their behalf?"

"*You* will give evidence on their behalf. If you wish, you may dress the part." This was followed by a guffaw.

Turning in a blaze of anger, masquerading as eccentricity: "Me? No matter how close to them I am, I am still outside."

24

The Rector took up a newspaper: "Look: *Itinerant Brawl Terrifies Villagers!*"

"Father Rector, can you name the Catholic dioceses in Nigeria?"

"Offhand, there's Onitsha, Owerri . . . Why?"

"We Irish send missionaries to the ends of the earth. But we have never made a positive attempt to speak charitably to ten thousand Irish outcasts!"

"That's what we're trying to do now."

"With that gang you call a Committee?"

"Now, now, Father Jim . . . That Committee meets on Saturday next at 241 St. Stephen's Green. . . . Ramble along and see what it's all about. I've phoned the Secretary and told him that you would be delighted to accept."

"You have?"

"Of course!"

"I see . . . yes, I see."

Remembering the conversation, Father Melody hobbled along. Number 241 should be over there somewhere. He thought of ten thousand people—fathers, mothers, nubile girls (the hands of the children blackberry-stained), old men and women scavenging, drinking, sleeping on road-sides, coughing up blood and phlegm, slatternish tots with their fingers up their noses ("Do you mind if I take your picture?" some of the passers-by asked), moving in a wicker-work of movement to and fro in Ireland, their matted hair an undergrowth beneath which they appeared to crouch. Faggot smoke cooked them like slit-open herrings. They were sick with drink slung into hollow bellies. Sweat impregnated their clothing: their babies rolled naked on frostbound roads while above and around them angry farmers swarmed.

And, with all that, little or no fornication, Father Melody told himself.

He walked past a farther line of seated students, their faces upturned to the sun.

He paused to look at a bed of snapdragons; then his head revolved to see that there was no park keeper in the vicinity. He plucked a bloom and squeezed on its throat until with a little sound the dragon opened its mouth.

(4)

Martin turned his eyes away from the sea, the Causeway, and the knot of tourists. He looked sidelong at his wife. "You feelin' all right?" he asked.

"What'd be wrong with me?"

"With the kid comin' any day, I thought you might be upset."

"Time come, child come!"

"After 'tis over, we'll head for home. We'll travel through the midland towns, avoidin' the *cuts* of other travellers. Two of us came up an' three of us'll go back."

He pondered for a while. " 'Tis August now," he said.

" 'Tis so!"

"Up to Puck Fair again."

"You're wishin' you were there?"

"I'm not."

"You're a liar!"

Martin did not answer.

"You're thinkin' of the women paradin' the streets o' Puck," Breda went on. "You're thinkin', too, of the women you had before you took up with me. Maybe you're thinkin' of one above the others."

"I'm not!" Martin said. "In the mornin' early when I

26

wake up in the camp, I sometimes think of Puck with its cheerin' as the goat is crowned. But it doesn't matter with me now as it did in days that are gone."

In Breda's eyes the embers of anger lost light.

"There's fun in Puck Fair, but not for me, the way I am." Her right hand tightened on her left to stop it trembling. "There's a black side to Puck, too."

"I seen your father struck by the McQueens. I seen him lyin' on the ground. 'Twas the first time I seen a man's brains oozin' through his skull."

As Breda shivered: "You're feelin' cold?" he asked.

"Up here, everythin' is cold: the winds, the sea, the islands, and the shore—they all smell like ice. The people here—their eyes are cold. 'Be off, you Fenian Papist beggars!'—that's what they say."

She drew the shawl about her.

Martin ran his palm backwards over her bleached hair.

"You're an old she-cat that's goin' to have kittens," he said. "I'm an old tomcat with the hair standin' on my back. How soon's your time?"

"Four days—five at the most."

"Are you right in your reckonin'?"

"I'm right!"

"What Mickle an' Poll-Poll an' myself keep tellin' you, is this: Look for a spike where you can born your child."

The girl half laughed. "A fellah in Galway had a drake on a griddle. When he'd put the music goin', he'd press an electric button an' the drake'd start to dance with the shocks it was gettin'. You remind me of that drake."

Martin looked rueful.

Again Breda laughed: "You'd take your oath 'twas you was givin' birth instead of me."

"A cat, a drake, what differ does it make?"

27

Breda faced him.

Suddenly, she ran her fingers up his face. She took his hand and brought its knuckles to her cheek, then lifted the broken-blue nails to her lips. "When I've my body back again, we'll have a second honeymoon," she said.

"Aye."

"Me an' you will make the bed of honour. An' we'll pretend it's our first time makin' it."

"You'd want to take no chances on the spike."

"That's printed on my brain," Breda said. She threw down his hand.

Martin walked away from her. "At most you have five days. Pick some place. Then I can be sure that both of ye will be safe."

"I showed you lots of spikes," he went on. "One had walls of red brick; another had beds on a roof as flat as my cart beyond. There was another spike, too, covered with roses."

"You showed me plenty spikes."

"If you're taken in the night, will you let Poll-Poll bring your child into the world?"

"I won't!"

"Wait so, till you're roarin' with your pains. . . ."

"I heard that before!"

"Poll-Poll might be sleepin' drunk. An' I'll have to wake up my stepfather, Mickle, to get him to scour the countryside for a midwife. An' here I'll be, listenin' to your screams."

Martin came closer. "Where is it you want to be confined?" he asked. "I'm tryin' to help you."

The girl rounded on him. "It was great help to drag me up the length of Ireland. Because you wanted to see what no Kerry tinker ever seen before—the top of Ireland!"

"You wanted that, the same as me!"

"I was happy where I was."

"That God may strike me dead! Comin' out of the chapel you whispered in my ear, 'We'll see places no Southern traveller ever seen before.'"

"No such words ever passed my lips," she said. "I begrudged every turn of the wheels that took me away from Kerry," she went on. "An' when I think that my kid'll see light far away from my own people, I'm fit to break my heart."

"What differ is there between spike an' spike? A bed to grip, a midwife to stand by—what else do you want?"

Martin was shouting jerkily, but his wife's voice rode him down.

"There's spikes is poxed with bad luck, an' the children out of 'em are born in bits. An' there's honey spikes, full of good fortune. Why did my mother lose her life? Because she picked an unlucky spike in Mayo. An' there she lost her babby an' herself. An' before she died . . ."

"She called you to her bed! 'Be sure to have your babbies in Dunkerron Spike,' she warned you, 'the one high in the hills above Kenmare. For it's a lucky spike, a honey spike . . .'"

"You're jeerin' me!"

"I'm not."

Her hands had become talons.

Martin rushed at her and tightened his arms around her. "That's what you told me do," he said, "if we fought. . . ."

For a moment she struggled frenziedly; then she lapsed against his breast.

He rocked her soothingly to left and right.

"Me an' Poll-Poll an' Mickle had to follow you," she

29

whined. "Maybe it would please you if I died, so that you'd see *her* face again?"

Martin was about to push his wife away; instead he drew her more closely to him.

"Me an' you, an' that's all!"

"You swear it?"

"I swear it."

Breda gripped the lapels of his coat and nuzzled her face against his breast. She shuddered. "It's as if someone walked across my grave," she whispered.

"Hush, woman."

"Take no notice of what I say."

"I won't," Martin said.

Breda raised her head and looked over his shoulder at the island riding on the water. A white sail had appeared at its western end. The girl groped in her memory to recall another island, now over three hundred miles away.

(5)

The seine-boat challenge had gripped the imagination of the southwest coast.

The McSweeneys of Ardoughter were seine-boat-born men. Thickset fishermen, they lived in limewashed cottages on an inlet of the sea that lay behind cliff walls.

The mouth of their miniature bay was like a gateway in stone. Through the gateway moved waves translucent with light.

The McSweeneys were clannish. Having beaten crews of older men at seine-boat racing, they grew proud.

A travelling photographer of Portuguese extraction had ridden his rusty bicycle into their hamlet and had seated the crew clan in rows at the pierhead. His professional eye told the photographer that the determined oarsmen, backdropped by the oars, the cliff gate, and the breakers, would make a good picture.

His camera in place, the little Portuguese fussed back and forth for a time and finally disappeared under the frayed black cloth. He held up his hand for attention: a moment later he declared that the photograph had been taken.

The McSweeneys glared at one another in disappointment; it was as if they had expected sweat and blood to follow such preliminaries.

But when the little Portuguese hopped out from the improvised darkroom in the hillside cottage and asked for clothes-pegs to hang up his prints, the glowering of the McSweeneys altered to smiling.

Mounted on white board with crimped edges, the pictures were impressive. They would look well hung up in the pubs of Camden Town of London, in the Bronx of New York, and in the Irish section of Melbourne.

Beneath each photograph was the legend: "The McSweeneys of Ardoughter, Ireland. Seine-boat champions of the world. All comers challenged."

By hell, the McSweeneys swore, this should make the O'Donnells on the other side of the Peninsula gripe with jealousy.

"Champions of the world!" the O'Donnells guffawed. "The McSweeneys wouldn't beat Katty Barry."

Their own seine boat was a heavy pot: racing with her was out of the question. So the O'Donnells wrote to the last of the O'Sullivan-Johns, a bus driver in Birmingham: "For the love of God, Jack, come home and build a racing seine boat that'll crush upstarts. Except for you and Rowlock, the craft is dead. And Rowlock is almost blind."

Jack O'Sullivan-John and his English wife and family laughed at the letter, though Jack's face, as he balled up the blue notepaper, showed something of reversion to Irish type. "What's a seine boat, Dad?" one of his sons asked. The boy had an English accent.

After waiting in vain for a reply, the O'Donnells called on Jack's uncle, old Rowlock. They steered him out into the sunlit field in front of his house.

"Before you die—one boat," they pleaded.

"I'm dark," the old man quavered.

"We'll give you six young eyes."

"I'm as dark as midnight," the old man said, but at last consented to make the boat.

From over cottage half-doors the O'Donnells watched the old man's trembling fingers move along the timbers where they were set out in the grass. The O'Donnell acolytes gave the blind man fingers and eyes. And, as counselled by their elders, they tried to learn the trade.

At last the boat was completed and tested. The blind boatbuilder stood in the wavelets of the strand, and five keen-sighted men told him how she rode the water.

The day the rival seine boats met at Bull Island was a memorable day along the southwest coast.

The tinkers of Munster were there in force. Breda, now twelve, was among them. Her father's death in a brawl had left her to the erratic mercy of an uncle.

The weather was fine; the island pier, the hotel balcony, the village street, the low fences of slate stone, and the road that stretched west swarmed with thousands of spectators.

Ferryboats pocked the air with sound as they brought cheering crowds to the island. "Up the O'Donnells!" "Up the McSweeneys!" the partisans roared.

In the tents, drinkers argued and roared. Now and again a man set down his glass and sang a ballad in praise of one of the two crews. As the time of the race approached, the buzz of the people took on a note of wildness.

The crews stripped to shirt and trousers, and donned the jerseys of their hurling teams. The mass of people crushed against the pier edges and darkened the rocks.

The two seine boats with their attendant boats moved out to the starting point in the bay. Behind and above them were the mountains of the peninsula. After the preliminaries came the puff of smoke from the starter's pistol.

As the sound of the shot reached the crowd, the people crackled into applause. Old Rowlock, seated on a fish box at the pierhead, asked a boy, in Gaelic, "Is she down at the prow?" Receiving the answer, "She's racin' level," the old man appeared satisfied.

Breda Claffey, squeezing through the throngs, had work to do. "Strike while the iron is hot" was the first lesson learned in begging. If everyone is facing east, you should face west. When caught off guard, people will fling you money.

So, threading through the roaring people on the pier, Breda, with a piping cry of, "Buy a tiepin, an' God bless you, sir!" gathered in the coppers. Some of the watchers glared into her face, then made atonement by moving their hands towards their pockets. There was the careless spilling of coins into her palm—anything to get rid of her while the race was in progress.

So, quick, quick while they're half mad! she urged herself. Hop, skip, and dodge forward! Make the most of the travellers' harvest. Before long, sanity and peasant miserliness will return. Then they'd refuse you the itch if they had two doses. Whine against their jerseys and whisper,

"God bless the O'Donnells!" or "God bless the lovely Mc-Sweeneys!"—this according to the clues offered by their conversation. Money—money—money—the weight of it increasing every minute in the string bag. "I have a fine trade," Breda told herself, "and all life is before me."

The smile died on her face as she saw Martin Claffey staring at her. She crinkled her face and stuck out her tongue at him

(6)

       "What do yeh think of the North?" Mickle asked. He nudged Poll-Poll with his elbow.

Mickle was driving the back-to-back car. Beside him, his wife, Poll-Poll, her eyes shut, crooned sleepily to herself.

The old woman belched. "The porter's poor!" she complained.

"It's not good," Mickle agreed. "Gee up!" he clucked to the black mare. The ribs of the animal shivered.

"Where did we say we'd meet 'em?" from Poll-Poll.

"West by the Causeway."

The old woman swayed tipsily. "You're a poor little stallion," she told Mickle.

"You met me when I was old."

"You were always old."

"I was in me tailboard!"

"The two men I was tied to before you would spit you out."

"They're dead, an' I'm alive!" Mickle dug his elbow into Poll-Poll's ribs, so that the old woman almost tumbled from the cart.

"You won't be alive if you do that to me again!"

Mickle began to sing:

"My love took down a German flute to play to me a tune,
And in the middle of the tune, my love to me did say:
'Molly, lovely Molly, I must leave you!' "

Mickle gave a loud yell and kissed the tattoo marks on the back of his hand; his huge nose made it difficult for him to get his lips to it. "I was a clean, smart soldier," he chortled.

Poll-Poll rocked with the swaying vehicle.

They drove east. The coast road switchbacked before them. Beside the roadway were great slabs of rock. Now and again they could see the white island on the water.

"The camel is an intelligent beast," Mickle Sherlock said. "He kneels down to get loaded. If you put too much on his back, he throws it sideways when he stands. Yehoo!" he shouted. "Up Karachi! Up Rawalpindi!"

Poll-Poll, her eyes closed, said, "You had women in the bizarres."

"Half the battalion of the Munster Fusiliers in hill stations at Gurraticka. The best of buffalo meat instead of cold Irish spuds. Me in a khaki shirt and shorts. Me wearin' a sun helmet marchin' to Mass. Me chasin' the Bataans at the p'int o' the bay'net into Afghanistan. Me, I say, playin' a hockey match after sundown in Karachi. Me with my mosquito curtain an' my fans in the Sudan. Me lyin' in bed, learnin' Hindustani. An' now, me here, tied to your dirty tail!"

"You were lyin' in the bizarres!"

"Mohammed Ali Square! Shepheard's Hotel! That hand

stretchin' out of a tent at mornin' to feel the hot sand under the Pyramids. Me now puttin' out my lousy hand on to the mucky edge of an Irish boreen."

Mickle stood up in the vehicle. "Major Tessard, sir! Colonel Johnson, sir!" he shouted.

"Coloured women are divils!"

Mickle pointed with his lash-topped crop out into the North Sea. "The Irrawaddy River!" he said. He pointed to the white sail. "A paddleboat movin' against the current. That's me, standin' on the deck, a toppin' soldier to catch loot-wallahs."

"You'd steal the nails out of a crucifix!"

"Nine days goin' up. Four days comin' down. The gongs soundin' all night in the temples. Pineapples galore in a hill village in the Andaman Islands." He laughed. "Andamanese women were small an' curlyheaded." He put his hand over his cupped nose. "Bully boys!" he yelled.

"I knew it wasn't the Rosary you were sayin'!"

"The parson mad, the padre madder; wild oranges everywhere; cheetahs jackin'-well eatin' our pet dogs; our knives an' forks crossed over our plates for fear the kite-hawks would snap our mate. 'See you in Ceylon, matey!' A G-string an' a leaf; the monsoon smokin' on the horizon. To hell with Ireland an' up the blazin' East! G'wan out, mare!"

"Diddle diddle dom-dom dee," Poll-Poll sang. After a while: "Where did you say we'd meet 'em?"

"At the Causeway. Hurry! The heifer'll drop the calf."

"That she might," Poll-Poll growled, "for fear she mightn't."

The swaybacked mare pricked up her ears and rocked on.

(7)

Martin drew his hatbrim down over his forehead. He took the gaggle of tin measures out of the cart. "I'll try the cottage beyond," he said.

Breda did not answer.

A seagull moved inshore and passed over them. Breda watched the bird's flight.

"The gull!" she said, in a low voice.

"Aye?"

"He's flyin' south. Supposin' that he's headin' for . . . ?"

"For where?"

"For the Kerry coast."

Martin stood watching the bird.

"An' supposin' that he flew straight across the land," Breda went on, "would it take him long to reach Kenmare?"

"What's on your mind?"

Breda laughed.

"Our cob, Tomboy, is on my mind. If he trotted at his best, how long would it take him to get to Kerry?"

"You seen Ireland on a postage stamp?"

"I did."

"That's the only bloody place it's small. Under a cob's hooves, it's big." A pause. "Why do you ask?"

"Nothin'."

"The cob that'd do three hundred and fifty miles in four days hasn't yet been foaled. What are you thinkin' about?"

"I'm thinkin' of Ballyheigue Castle lookin' across the bay. An' of Tralee where the marketwomen sell cockles.

I'm thinkin', too, of the fuchsia flowers along the Dingle road."

"Is that all?"

"No. I'm thinkin' of Coumeenole Strand where, after we were married, me an' you went swimmin'."

"You're thinkin' of the spike above Kenmare!"

"I am!"

"Put it out of your head." He made to move off. "Stay here till Mickle an' Poll-Poll come. Tell 'em I won't be long."

Breda waited till he was close to the cart. Then she shouted, "I'm goin' to Kerry for my babby to be born."

"You're foolin'."

"I'm in earnest. Sit into the flat cart an' we'll be off."

"I won't!"

"If I don't born my child in Dunkerron, I'll lose my life."

"You'll lose no life."

In a few swift steps, Breda was beside him. "My mother called me in the night," she said.

"That tantrum will pass."

"I have four or five days. Hurry, I tell you!"

"If I had the fastest horse in Ireland, I'd never reach that spike in time."

Breda gripped his sleeve. "I'll not let go the child till we get to the place. We can cross into the Republic in the dark. There'll be no police around. It's a straight run down through Ireland then. Keep away from Puck Fair an I'll be right. If Mickle an' Poll-Poll don't want to follow us, let 'em go to hell. Hurry, Martin, boy."

He wrenched his sleeve out of her fingers. "I'll go no-place," he said.

"Mickle will drive me!"

"His spavined animal can barely walk."

"I want my child to be born where I told you." She turned. The chime of harness bells reached her ears.

Breda swung to face her husband. "If you do as I say, I'll give you happiness with my mind—and my body, too."

The harness bells came closer. "An' if you don't give in, I'll make your life a hell."

The knuckles of Breda's fingers showed white as she clung to her husband. Martin asked himself when it was she had clung to him like that before.

He too then recalled the island and the day of the boat race.

(8)

The boats were halfway to the turning point. The cheering had grown abandoned.

"A copper, for the love of God," Breda begged, ending the pretence of selling from her basket. She inched out to where huge limestones marked the pier edge; there she had bare body and basket room.

Savagery had taken possession of the crowd.

The tonal quality of the cries made Breda glance out to sea. The boats were approaching the buoy that marked the turning point of the race; with a burst of speed the O'Donnell boat rounded the mark and drew away from its rival.

The McSweeneys put all their strength into a frenzied rhythm of rowing that sent their boat pivoting on the buoy and quickly brought them level with their opponents. Suddenly the two sets of oars locked and both seine boats stopped in a swirl.

The banging of timber noised across the water. The attendant boats closed in. The rival crews were on their feet shouting wildly; they began to grip one another. The satellite boats joined in the fray. Soon the black knot in midsound showed flying fists and raised oars. Men standing rocked the craft dangerously.

The cries of the men at sea enraged the onlookers on the pier, who had begun to sway backwards and forwards in time with the fight. As an oar, ponderously swung, described a downward arc among the combatants, the crowd on the pier surged forward.

Breda was tossed out and down into the sea ten feet below her.

She came up with her mouth open. She uttered a yelp of outrage and terror. Her head, with the hair plastered close to her scalp, seemed attenuated. Her eyes were dilated. She resembled a kitten, accustomed only to a fireside, that has been flung into an icy pool. For a time her clothes proved buoyant; she remained semi-afloat as, also, did the basket and the shawl.

The crowd paid her scant attention.

The men above her were arguing loudly. Breda's body, then her head, went underwater. The head came up, her mouth barely able to utter a gurgling scream. The basket swayed to the bottom. Red baize Sacred Heart badges were left on the surface of the water. A few seconds later the shawl had disappeared.

Again Breda went down and again came up yelling frenziedly.

"Look at the tinker kid!" someone shouted.

"Swim, monkey!" another cried.

The majority of the spectators were indifferent to her plight.

As she found the water weighing down her clothes, Breda began to scream in despair.

40

Martin Claffey heard the screams. He dodged among the throng until he reached the pier edge; there he pushed his head between the thighs of two fishermen. Below him he saw the crazied face. He shrugged off his long coat, and leaped, boots foremost, into the sea. In the natural way a dog swims he fought his way to the girl's side and clutched her hair.

She turned towards him and, crying and gulping spasmodically, wound her hands and legs about him; she put her open mouth against his face as if preparing to fasten her teeth in his features or clothes. Martin fought himself free.

Again he approached her; again she clutched him close. For a moment they were two rats in grotesque embrace; then Martin beat the girl in the face with his fist until she released her hold. He pushed-clawed her to the point where the slip slid into the water.

A gnarled old fellow, wearing spectacles, walking down the slip, said, "Come up ou'r that!"

Crouching, he caught Martin by the gansey and slewed him around. Martin brought Breda with him so that both lay panting on the rounded stones of the slipway. A wash from the sea took them.

Martin got slowly to his feet. In the struggle his belt had slipped and his breeches had fallen down around his knees. As he made to move upwards on the slip, the breeches fettered him, so that he staggered against the wall and fell backwards on his rump.

Again he struggled to his feet. He looked like a weary retriever that had been long fetching from a marsh. The people above jeered as he dragged up his trousers and made his way upwards on to the pier. He did not look back at the sprawled figure of the girl.

At sea, the combatants had been separated. In one of the boats a man stood up and faced the shore. "Justice!" he shouted, his voice carrying across the water.

The man with the owlish eyes who had dragged Martin out of the sea stepped after an ebbing wave and looked down at the prone body of Breda. He turned her over with his shoe sole and then prodded her with his toecap.

She came dismally to her hands and knees, clawed the setts, and then tensed to lean against the pier wall. Here she puked water. After a time she came erratically upright. Her nose was bleeding. She took a step forward, stopped, half turned in the reeling water, and then, recalling her basket and shawl, began to howl. On a thought she clasped her thigh and reassured herself that her string purse was safe. This fact comforted her a little.

Water pouring from her clothes, she staggered upwards. Too cowed to curse those who laughed at her, she hobbled through the multitude. She then realised that she had lost her shoes in the sea.

Snivelling and running her wrist under her nostrils, she moved to the pierhead. The crowd parted to let her through. She bumped into the blind boatmaker; he drew a blow of his stick across her shoulder blades. She squealed and began to run, leaving a trail of water behind her.

Where the crowd was less dense, she slowed to a walk. Reaching the roadway, she scuffed her bare feet in the dust and shuffled south along the coast road.

Once she turned and looked across the sound. There was no way of getting to the camp on the mainland: the ferryboats were moored at the slip and the ferrymen were taken up with the hullabaloo of the broken race.

As she walked onwards, the heat of the sun penetrated

her sodden clothes and warmed her skin. After travelling for the most of a mile, she stopped.

The far din of the thousands came to her; she looked up and down the road. No one. She squeezed between the roots of two whitethorn bushes on the fence and dropped into a field. She made her way uphill. Her fingers kept pushing the lank hair out of her eyes. Reaching the hill-top, she stopped before a cover of bracken and furze that marked the site of a broken earth fort.

From here she could see the people milling around the pier, the striped tents, and the boats, which now seemed insignificant on the spread of the sound. Across the water were the mountains of the mainland.

As she went round the earthwork of the fort, a flock of sheep ran bleating before her. Spying a gap in the thorn-bushes, she wriggled through. Inside the fort was a space where, among the bracken stems, the grass had been close-cropped by the sheep. The place was a trap of sun heat. She stood in an alleyway in the bracken, listening care-fully. She heard the grasshopper snipping. She saw the blue-green needle of the dragonfly holding a single spot of air. She inhaled deeply.

Looking around her like a wary animal, she sank to her knees. She pulled tufts of soft grass and, spitting on them, did her best to clean her bloodied and bruised face. She then peeled off her clothes, squeezed them, and spread them on the bracken to dry. She clasped her hands across her tiny breasts, shuddered, and then, her eyes still darting here and there, lay down and curled herself up.

The blow of the boatbuilder's stick had left a weal across her shoulder blades.

For a time, she shivered. Gradually her body eased in

the heat of the sun. Before she fell asleep she started, as a dog starts in dream. "Claffey!" she said, with venom, and then snivelled in self-pity.

Her mouth tightened as she recalled his heel poised above her play bird and his brown eyes hard with anger. Then she remembered the same eyes confronting her in the water. Gradually her mouth relaxed.

Before she fell asleep, she had begun to smile.

(9)

"I'm damned as low as Lucifer," Mickle said.

Waddling past Martin and Breda, he glared down at the Causeway. He dropped heavily to the grass and sat with his back against a paling post.

"A fella shook hands with me, an' I comin' out of a pub," Mickle went on. " 'You're a loyal servant of the Queen,' says he. Me, that turned Republican after I sold me British Army pension! 'A true blue,' says he, 'so me an' you will scarify the Pope an' then we'll drink the health of King William victor of the Boyne.' God forgive me, I drank with him. . . .

"Every time I said somethin' outrageous, I winked at myself in a mirror. Out with me in the street. A constable came up: 'Your name?' says he. 'My name?' says I. An' I was goin' to . . ."

"But you didn't!" Poll-Poll said.

She, too, had squatted against the fence.

" 'You're over the border from the State?' says the constable," Mickle went on. " 'The state of grace,' says I. 'None of your lip!' says he. 'My two lips,' says I. That flattened him. An' I was goin' to tell him to his teeth . . ."

"All a bantam cock has is his crow," Poll-Poll said.

A grin spread over Mickle's face. "There was trouble at the border last night," he said. "D'ye hear? The IRA's are at it again. We from the South would want to watch our step."

The old tinker took off his greasy hat and began to fan his face.

"Hey!" Poll-Poll shouted at Martin as if Breda were not present. "That wife o' yours—did she pick a spike?"

"Aye!"

"Would it be far from here?"

Martin did not answer.

"I'd say it's a long step from here," Mickle said, his eyes on Breda's face.

"Is it Cookstown or Omagh?" Poll-Poll asked Breda.

"Dunkerron's where the babby'll be born," Breda said.

"Dunkerron below in Kerry?" Mickle laughed. "That's three or four hundred miles away. That's not the place you mean?"

"That same!"

" 'Tis the babby after this she means," Mickle told the others. "Or the babby that's beyond that babby still." He drew the inside of his hat across his face.

"How'll you get there?" Poll-Poll asked. "Spread your shawl an' fly?"

"I'll travel in my own flat," Breda said. "I won't trust my life to your dirty paws, nor neither to unlucky spikes. An' I dar' any of ye to stop me!"

"You're crazy, girl!" Mickle said. "If we crossed the border safely, the Midland farmers'd take our lives. An', if we dodged those boyos, the travellers of Middle Ireland would gut us."

"Ye heard me!" Breda said. "I won't rest until I'm inside the walls of the hospital in Dunkerron.

"Tackle the cob an' we'll be off," she told Martin. "Tackle the cob, or I'll bare my breast an' curse ye!"

"I won't go!" Martin said.

"Nor me!" Poll-Poll said. She lumbered to her feet.

Mickle paused for a moment. He extended his arms to the full and pointed at the sky. The three others looked up as if expecting to see a vision riding the vehicles of the heavens. His arms still spread, he came to his feet. "Steady!" he said.

"Did the sun rise yesterday?" he went on. "It did. Did it rise today? It did. Will it rise tomorrow? It will. But it will also rise on a day when none of us will be alive to see its light. Here, damn the devil an' his wooden leg, I vote we go!"

With a push, Poll-Poll sent him sprawling. "My hands brought more than a hundred childer into the world," she told Breda. "I'll handle you so that, while a cat'd be lickin' her ear, your child will be in the crook of your arm."

"You'll born no child o' mine," Breda cried.

She wrenched the whip from Martin's boot. Drawing it back over her shoulder, "By the face of Christ, if you don't come with me . . . ," she shouted. She made as if to strike the old woman across the face.

Martin caught the lash and jerked the whip out of his wife's hands.

Breda cried out at the pain of her abraded fingers. Throwing off her shawl, she sprang to where the wire fence joined a dyke of clay. Staggering upwards on the dyke, she stood above them, swaying. "If you don't go with me," she screamed, "I'll jump. Then the kid will be born in pulp."

"Come off that fence!" Martin shouted.

"Let her jump to hell!" Poll-Poll said.

"If ye don't take me to Kerry, I'll pitch myself down."

Breda tottered and almost lost her balance. As Martin and Mickle approached, "Don't come another step," she screamed.

Martin and Mickle stood irresolute.

(10)

"Lass!"

Breda vaguely realized that someone was calling her from below.

She looked down and saw an old woman dressed in black trundling up along the pathway from the shore. "Lass! Lass!" the woman called in a North of England accent.

Breda screamed at the top of her voice, "If ye don't take me this minute, down I'll go!"

Her eyes on the hysterical girl, the woman below urged herself against the incline. Reaching the wicket gate, she gripped the handrail, looked at the tinkers, and said, gaspingly: "Of course, they'll take you, lass. Coom down off the fence and chat wi' me."

No one spoke. "That they'll do," the woman wheedled. "Coom down, lass."

Breda's breathing was audible. Her eyes dilated as she glanced at the newcomer.

"You her husband?" the woman asked.

Martin hitched the cans higher on his shoulder.

"Will you take your wife where she wants to go?"

"No!" Poll-Poll shouted.

"Wasn't speakin' to you," the woman said.

Breda began to scream, a high-pitched animal scream.

"Gi' me your hand, lass, and tell me what's wrong." Inch by inch, the Englishwoman approached the tinker girl. She extended a bunch of throttled flowers. "Come doon and look at mah flowers," she said.

Still breathing heavily, Breda looked at the newcomer.

"Flowers are people," the old woman said. "See, they have faces like you and me. They're old and young, happy and sad. Has no one told you that before?"

Her eyes fast on the flowers, Breda's body went limp. She placed her fingertips on the old woman's upturned palm. "If I stay here to have my kid, I'll die," she moaned. "I'll go to Dunkerron, even if I littered on the road."

"Of course you will," said the Englishwoman. "But come doon first. That's it, lass."

Dreamily, Breda stepped off the fence. "Somewhere for your bairn to be born?" the Englishwoman probed.

"Aye!"

To Martin, "You are her husband?"

"Yes."

"Take your wife in the cart and drive her where she wants to go."

"I own to God!" Poll-Poll yelled, her features knotted in anger.

Breda had begun to whimper. The Englishwoman released the girl's hand and set the choked flowers on the grass. She turned to face the tinkers.

"When Ah was young," she said, "the name of Meg Postlethwaite was feared in 'Bowton' an' in Bootle. Ah've held mah own in the cotton mills, wi' ugly women an' wi' uglier men. Ah bit the ear off a weaver who tried to rape me. An' spat it on the ground—ah did! An' ah led mah Union in a dirty strike—an' won it, too. Sit in your carts before ah do you harm."

The chocolate-coloured shawl half slid from Poll-Poll's

shoulders. Her powerful brown hands closed into mis-shapen fists.

"Sit in your cart, you silly drunken Irish bitch!" Meg cannonaded.

"I'll swing for you!" Poll-Poll shouted.

Moving aside, Meg allowed Poll-Poll to swing past her. As she careered past, the Englishwoman struck the tinker with her fist on the back of the neck. The blow was sufficient to send Poll-Poll head foremost into the clay fence.

Martin dropped his tin measures and rushed forward. As the Englishwoman grabbed a bit of paling post to defend herself, Breda hurled herself upon her and, snatching the weapon, flung it over the cliff.

With the force of Breda's unexpected attack, Meg collapsed awkwardly beside Poll-Poll. The old tinker woman swung sideways and began to pummel her.

Mickle tore the women apart.

"Come on!" he cried, shaking his wife. "Sit into the cart an' we'll gain as much ground as we can in front of 'em. We're goin' to Kerry, d'ye hear?"

He dragged Poll-Poll uproad. The old woman was full of maudlin fight.

"Watch for the grass I'll throw at the crossroads,' Mickle shouted. "That'll tell you where we've gone. If you see a red rag tied to a bush, skedaddle like the wheels of hell."

"Do as yer woman tells you," Mickle shouted at Martin. Turning to the girl: "He'll go, Breda. You'll see." Again he shouted at Martin: "You've seen the top of Ireland now—what more d'you want? Into the carts with ye! My oul' mare will match it step for step with the cob. Come on, Martin! Right or wrong, don't you fail a woman caught in a hoult!"

Martin turned and looked at his wife. She was tight-lipped and pale; her cheekbones were straining the skin of her face. He looked at his mother and noted, as for the first time, her saffron eyes, her half-open mouth, and her tipsy crouch. He looked at the sycophantic face of Mickle.

Over his head the gull cried—once, twice. Martin looked up at the circling bird. He then looked down at the shore, the island, and the sea.

He crouched to pick up the tin measures. "All right!" he said. Indicating his wife, "If there's trouble at the end of the road, she can sup her sorrow with a long spoon!"

Mickle and Poll-Poll had begun to sway towards their cart. Martin moved slowly in the direction of his own cart. He swung the cans into the body of the vehicle; he then loosed the reins and leaped lightly onto the side of the cart.

"Back, Tomboy!" he yelled.

Poll-Poll grabbed the crupper of the mare and ponderously lifted her knee. Mickle crouched, got his shoulder under his wife's rump, and pushed her up.

Swinging her shawl about her, Breda clambered into her husband's cart. Martin looked up at the sun, then slashed the animal with his whip.

"Go on out, Tomboy!" he roared.

Still seated on the ground, the old Englishwoman wryly watched them go. Then she groped for her flowers, and lumbered slowly to her feet.

TWO

The way it is in Ireland, there were always
  restless men
Who said the Island should be one and the loaf
  be whole again
—The Tinkers crossed the Border by a road
  that lacked a pike
And blood was spilled in the moonlight as they
  raced for the Honey Spike.

(1)

"I'm thinkin' of somethin' all day," Breda said, with a glance at her husband.

Martin said nothing.

Resting on her heels she bent over a fire on which a pan, containing a mixum-gatherum of victuals, crackled. Hanging from a snapped-off branch, a Tilley lamp shed a harsh light on the scene.

Martin, on his feet, was lying against the fence, out of range of the fire and lamplight.

Breda moved the blade of a knife deftly among the contents of the frying pan.

They were encamped on a road edge above a long valley that had narrowed to a ravine. The canvas of the semicircular camp showed green in the lamplight. High in the night sky dark clouds were rimmed by the light of a concealed moon. The cloud packs, high and monstrous, added a bizarre dimension to the night world.

"As we were travellin'," Breda went on, "I was workin' my hips back an' forth. I had the queer notion that I was the cob between the shafts." She laughed softly.

Briars clung to Martin's coat as he pulled away from the fence. He tightened his belt a notch and stood listening. He then picked up a head collar from the grass. The bit rattled and flashed in the lamplight. Martin moved away a few steps and again paused to listen.

Breda glanced sharply up at him. For a moment or two she seemed about to check her urge to speak. Then she began, "I'm thinkin' of puttin' a piece on my head an' pretendin' that I'm a gypsy who can see what's hidden an' to come."

Stretching out her left hand and cupping it slightly as if holding a girl's hand palm upwards, she began to mimic the fortune-telling of a gypsy:

"A tall dark man in a Government house has the wish of his heart for you, my lovely girl. An' here's a letter with money in it comin' from across the sea. But wait! I see the face of a false friend, who has the initial J . . . or K . . ."

Breda broke off in laughter.

"I tried it once," she said, "at the Fair of Toghar. Then a priest gave a sermon an' set the parish at my heels!"

She laid the knife on the pan edge, and snatched the kerchief from around her throat. Deftly she arranged the kerchief on her head and held it at the nape of her neck so that she resembled a gypsy.

"This is the way I was!" she said.

When she saw her husband's set face, the kerchief went loose. She drew it down limply.

Gripping the knife handle, she began to stab at the victuals.

Somewhere in the valley the wind rattled leaves.

Martin slung the head collar into the cart. He walked to the crown of the narrow road. Behind him the blade tip noised thoughtfully in the pan.

Martin strode downroad. Trees interlaced their branches over his head. He came to where a series of iron spikes had been set in a concrete base that ran across the roadway: the barrier ended in two concrete piers—one on each road margin. Each spike was a light girder hacksawed across at an angle so as to make a rough point. The points inclined towards the border of the Republic, which lay some distance downroad.

With a blow of the heel of his hand, Martin struck one of the spikes near the point. The steel thrummed.

The tinker made a sound indicative of satisfaction. Standing between a pair of spikes, he peered into the darkness beyond the barrier. He then examined the barrier from different angles, as if estimating how he would get his cart over or through it. He went to the concrete pier on the road margin above the valley. Above it was a black-and-white notice.

Martin screwed up his eyes. On the notice was a crown with two large words underneath it. The printing was well done. That meant that it was a Government notice. Together notice and barrier said: Get to hell out of here!

Martin looked back in the direction of the camp. First thing he'd do when he got back was to lower the lamp.

He moved behind the pier and looked across the clay fence into the sloping meadow. Somewhere, Tomboy was tearing at the grass. In a long window on the opposite side of the valley was an oblong of light. To Martin it appeared to be the window of a Government building—probably a police barracks with sandbags set on the sills inside.

A yelp from Breda made Martin turn. He returned quickly to the fire. "What's wrong?" he asked.

"Somethin' darted across there!"

"Ach!—only a rat!"

"Aye!" Then, "Is the cob all right?"

"He's all right."

"You fettered him?"

"Yes."

"Not with a chain?"

"No! With a rope."

She tumbled part of the contents of the pan onto a cracked enamel plate. Martin lowered the lamp a little, then squatted on the ground opposite her. He took off his hat, set it on the grass, and began to pick up scraps of food with his fingers. Breda set down the pan at the edge of the fire and began to eat from the enamel plate. She broke off eating to tear a loaf in two and hand her husband the larger portion. Now and again, at the fire's edge, a burning faggot exploded with a spurt of grey ashes.

Eating, Breda's movements were delicate; she did not take a portion until Martin had first drawn food from the plate. When the plate was almost empty, she slopped what remained on the pan onto it. The meal at an end, Martin wiped his fingers in his hair.

"There's another board at the barrier," he said.

Breda sopped up the sector of the plate nearest her with the soft side of a crust of bread.

After a pause, he began again: "The time you spent in the orphanage after your ma an' da died—didn't they teach you how to read?"

"I can read small words."

"The words on this notice are big. Small words or big— they're all the same to me."

"It's a drawback to be that way."

"It's a God's curse."

"Aye."

"If I was able to read the names over the shops itself," Martin said. "If it's the last thing I do, I'll see that *he* reads."

"I'll help you to see that *he* reads," Breda said.

"About the shops," she began after a time: "The names are mostly in capitals."

"Capitals?"

"The big letters. I'd be a short time teachin' you what I know. After you're level with me in knowledge, we could find another way of gettin' more."

"I'd like to be able to read what's on a poster in a window," he said. "Or about the horse races an' the hurlin games in the newspapers. It's bad to be blind of half the world. Always signin' my name with a bloody oul' X. If I live to draw the Old Age Pension, I'll sign that with a cross too. That cross will be with me always—except it won't be over my grave."

She licked the tip of the knife, then wiped the blade on her skirt.

"Twenty-six letters in all," she said: "twice your fingers an' six with it."

She put up her spread fingers twice, then showed six fingers. He looked at her in surprise.

"Every word in the world can be made by those twenty-six letters," she went on.

"Surely there's more than twenty-six different words in the mouth of man?"

"The letters are bunched—a couple for a short word, more for a long word."

"Oh!"

"If I taught you one letter a day, you'd have the alphabet off in a month."

"What's an alphabet?"

"The list of the letters. Me an' you could have fun travellin' through Ireland, readin' what we seen printed. The whole country would be a book. . . . Martin! I'll start now! Raise the lamp."

He did so.

Breda pivoted on her knees and squatted at his feet. She patted the bare clay by his boots. With the knife she cut a crude *M* on the earth.

"That's *M*," she said. "Say it now."

"Em!"

"It's like a gate that's closed between you and me. *M!* Look how I made it. *M* for man, for mange—what a dog gets—for music, for mother, for Martin." She smiled up at him. "*M* says Muh-muh-muh-Martin. That's what the old nun used to say in the Home."

"*M!*" he said, looking down at the letter with a childlike interest. He came slowly down till his buttocks rested on his heels. "*M!*" he said, with concentration and satisfaction. He traced the letter with his index finger. "That's one letter I'll know if I see it in a public house."

"Almighty God!" she said, "you're lookin' at it upside-down. To you that way it's *W—W* for watch, for water, for woman . . ."

"How could it be *M* and the other thing at the same time?"

"It's accordin' to the way you look at it. This way it's *M* an' that way it's *W*. D'you see?"

"Book readin' is crazy!" Martin said. "Let it go to the devil!"

He came sharply to his feet.

(2)

When first he looked around the Dublin chemist's shop in which he had been appointed assistant, Frank Horan had smiled at its quaintness.

"Here I'll likely be asked for leeches," he told himself with a smile.

Yet, country boy though he was, with the passing of time the old-fashioned place in the narrow street near Amiens Street Station had grown on him.

Especially he loved it when the sun struck down through the coloured water in the medieval carboys in the window. On the tiled floor the sunlight left daubs of colour, edged with rainbows that filtered through the prisms of the glass stoppers.

"Character!" Frank often breathed to himself when he looked around him in the Medical Hall. "Character!" he had also told himself when first he had set eyes on the proprietor of the place.

The man was small, lame, and pale; he carried himself with an old-world dignity that contrasted with his grog-blossomed nose.

"Young man!" John McAlinden, M.P.S.I., had said, "I have great respect for that pedagogue, your father. We are old friends. Yet he may not be aware that, of latter years, I am attached to . . ." He raised his hand quickly to his lips. "You understand?"

"I understand!"

"Not a word! Agreed?"

"Agreed!"

"When you become accustomed to the Hall and have mastered the arcanae of compounding, I shall, almost imperceptibly, delegate my authority to you."

Frank nodded.

"Ah!" from old McAlinden. Like a terrier yapping: "You, yourself, are not addicted to . . . ?" He half raised his hand.

"I don't drink."

"Couldn't stand it if both ends of the house were on fire." With pride: "I am the last of a great line of compounding chemists in this city. I trace my professional descent from a chemist to Dean Swift. You will find my skill, sporadically though it may be exercised, admirable."

59

After this, proprietor and assistant got on well together.

The passage of time had also reconciled Frank to city life and to the anonymity of city lodgings.

There were days when, on looking out over the compounding screen of the Hall, he fancied he could see the sheep grazing on the mountain above his Kerry home.

Even the ornamental jar of olives on one of the shelves reminded him of his schoolmaster father telling barefooted hill children of the agony of Christ in Gethsemane.

Yet these fancies were offset by the craftsman's love McAlinden had aroused in him. Frank came to cherish mortar and pestle, the ranked glass jars, and the mahogany chest of drawers bearing black legends on golden arc-scrolls.

These are my two worlds, Frank told himself: the brown-gold factual world of the shop: the blue-green dream world of hills and lakes.

But at times he had to admit to the existence of a third world, the world that had to do with the knitting together of the two parts of a broken island, the world of historical figures whispering that the conquest was not yet undone.

My third world may kill me, if I do not kill it, Frank told himself.

He took off his glasses and began to polish them. If you wore spectacles with thick lenses, you were considered as something of an idiot. People who looked at you (because they failed to see the eye pupils) thought they themselves could not be seen. At times they grimaced as if in the presence of a fool.

A determined knocking with a coin on a glass case brought him out from behind the screen.

"Well, son?" he asked the gamin customer.

(3)

There had also been a ravine beyond the fence and arched trees downroad, Breda remembered, on the night Martin and she had first talked about marrying.

In retrospect, she could clearly see the dark roadside beyond the bridge where the two campfires had burned low. The fires were fifty or sixty paces apart; around each circle of embers a group of tinkers squatted in silence.

Interspersed with goats and dogs, heaps of iron and mattresses, a line of caravans and carts stretched away on the road edge from each of the two fires.

From time to time each tinker group, almost as a unit, raised its head and glared in the direction of the other.

Downroad a cob clanked its fetters. Carried on a shift of wind, the brawling of the river was held.

The first leaf of autumn fell.

In one of the fireside groups a child giggled—Mickle Sherlock scowled it to shame. By the other fire a girl of thirteen or so sighed; a young man glanced sharply at her.

Suddenly a boy of ten came to his feet. He looked towards the point of deep darkness where the trees were arched above the road.

The knock of shoes was heard. Footsteps were heard approaching. Martin came first, his hands deep in his fob pockets. Moving closely behind his shoulders, Breda followed.

Martin passed the fire at which his mother, Poll-Poll, and his stepfather, Mickle Sherlock, sat among his relatives. The girl still behind him, he sauntered on. He halted at a point equidistant from the Claffey and Gilligan fires.

Taking his right hand from his pocket, he flicked his hat-brim upwards.

The tension caused by the arrival of the young pair was somehow felt beyond the two encampments where, on the higher ground at the other side of the bridgehead, a farther file of nondescript vehicles was drawn up on the margin of the road.

Here were gypsies and horse copers, circus roustabouts, pick-and-win merchants, ballad singers, memory men, durrackers or fortune-tellers, and buskers of all sorts.

Mickle glanced at Poll-Poll; he then looked from one to the other of the faces of the men around him.

As a growl was heard, Mickle came to his feet. "Stay where you are!" Poll-Poll muttered tipsily.

Adopting the begging shuffle he usually reserved for outsiders, Mickle went to where Breda and Martin stood. As if making a protective cross with his body, he extended his arms.

The men of both encampments stirred uneasily. The women stared down at the fires. This taking of a girl from her campfire and walking her off into the darkness should and would be paid for. If this law was broken, who knows but the roads would be black with *lospairts*.

The younger girls pushed their faces against their mothers' shoulders; their eyes, like those of fox cubs, took in the details of the scene. The eyes of the boys shone with immature fighting lust. The mongrels' manes bristled.

"No trouble!" Mickle shouted.

In the gypsy territory the people stood waiting.

Winifred McQueen came down the steps of her wagon. Following the gaze of the others, she saw Martin and Breda standing between the two fires. As she walked forward a few steps, the men looked at her eagerly; the women looked at her with jealousy and hatred mingled.

"Did you make a man of him?" a hag whispered. Winifred laughed. "He's caught a heifer calf," the old woman said, shading her eyes to look at Martin and Breda.

Downroad the young pair stood without movement.

Martin's suit was new, a black and yellow scarf was loosely knotted about his neck. Beneath her bright dress, Breda's body was unbound; a red and orange shawl hung around her left shoulder.

The second leaf of autumn fell.

At the Gilligan fireside a dirty-faced girl pushed an ashcrop closer to the searching hand of one of Breda's uncles.

In the other group a boy fumbled behind him until his fingers met a kettle bar. This he began secretly to work towards a redheaded giant who resembled Martin.

As on a signal, the two tinker groups came to their feet and began to pad softly towards where Martin, Breda, and Mickle stood.

(4)

"By the holy fiddle!" Father Melody said, addressing his reflection in the window of the railway carriage in which he sat alone, "I never thought of that before."

Beyond the glass, the fields of the Midlands rushed past.

"That'll shake the Holy Insulars in their combinations!" the priest went on. "It will be a shock for the lads in tonsure suits who want life in boxes like marzipan sweets!"

"By hell!" he said, in a louder tone, "one of their own

could redeem these rascals. A towhead with an alert brain reaching out into the world of abstract thought . . . And, all the while, his eyes, maybe, recalling roadside fires. Aloof, growing and withdrawn. Alone, as only the priest is alone."

Come to think of it, the Jesuit told his reflection, there *was* a society that handled the vocation of indigent yet earnest youths. Listed on the back pages of pious magazines were burses to burn. Good, begod!

This boy he had in mind was as yet unknown. Even now, immaturely, the lad's mind was on the illimitable. And he, Father James Anthony Melody, would come to hear of him and would write a letter on his behalf to the Father Provincial.

Dear John, I know that it may sound appalling to ask you to consider a vocation from such a depressed section of the Community (if, indeed, "travellers" form part of the community at all) but I think that this may be the solution to their problems.

If this boy proves worthy, he may raise them from the clay—John! to hell with cant like this—get those pinprick-minded doctrinarians to release the jack necessary to tog out this kid and send him to the Seminary.

Barbarous? Inconceivable?

Did you ever find me interested in anything that wasn't barbarous and inconceivable? I know! Unless God, aided and abetted by you and me, intervenes, but pronto, many will be lost.

You may say, as you have said before, that the day that they clapped a Roman collar on James Anthony Melody and told him that, by the blue blazes, he'd better practice prudence or would live to rue it, was a doleful one in the

annals of the Roman Catholic Church in the Island of
Saints and Scholars.

John! I want a young tinker togged out for the Seminary
of All Saints. And if I don't get my way, I'll raise the roof.

The fancy grew in Father Melody's imagination.

His Right Reverence the President would press his nose
to the leaded windows of his study, his eyes goitrous with
dismay. For he had just heard that caravans, flat carts, and
a fleet of vehicles—all in disrepair—had assembled at the
crossroads below the village.

And that the public houses of the village—Burke's and
Hanrahan's—had been drunk dry by a jostling assembly of
tinker men, tinker women, and tinker babies-in-arms—
these last preferring the taste of unracked whiskey to the
taste of breast milk. What a scandal to the relatives of the
other ordinandi!

Alleluia! Father Melody chuckled, the glorious riffraff of
the land assembled in the paddocks of Kildare to see a son
of nature ordained according to the Order of Melchiz-
edech.

The train stopped at a wayside station. Father
Melody remained seated, blissfully looking through the
window. His smile was so broad that porters and bystanders began to smile broadly, too.

. . . and, Lord God of Hosts! after the ceremony, the
young priest walking among clan and counterclan, his fingers, that on the morrow would conjure Christ into the ac-
cidents of a bread sliver, smooched with spittle after they
had been kissed and licked by the barely sober throng
scuffling forward on their knees for the blessing.

A bloody fine impish fancy, Father Melody told himself.

"And, by the Fly of Thebes!" he added, aloud, "one worthy of me!"

A porter opened the carriage door. "You're gettin' out here, aren't you, Father?"

Father Melody glanced at the notice board at the station. "Shalloo," it said. Was it Shalloo? Or Buttevant or Ballydehob?

He found his ticket—yes, it was Shalloo.

"Almost missed it!" he said. "Never do to have all those Franciscans clack into chapel for their annual retreat and find the Jesuit *non est*. Shalloo? View-halloo! This certainly is the station for the monastery."

As he made his way to the waiting pony and trap, he asked himself how the devil the porter knew.

(5)

> Out of breath, her hair in greasy coils, Poll-Poll lurched up the roadway on the Republic side of the border. Squeezing through the teeth of the barrier, she rested her hands on the shafts of the cart and eyed Martin and Breda.

The light of the Tilley lamp brought warmth to her faded chocolate shawl.

"Are ye two mad?" she asked.

"Why?" from Breda.

"Did ye see the trail o' grass on the road?"

"We followed it here."

"An' no farther? Heart o' God! Did ye see the red rag I tied to the bush beyond?"

Belatedly, Martin's eyes caught the rag.

" 'Twas dark when we got here," Breda said.

"The camp is up," Martin said. "The cob is fettered in the meadow. We're goin' to sleep. Off with you!"

Poll-Poll spat phlegm on the grass. "Ye're on the border, d'ye hear?" she said. "This is the hottest shop in Ireland. The place is alive with smugglers an' with bombin' IRA's."

"Off with you to the fella that took my father's bed," Martin said lightly.

"I got a clown in you!" Poll-Poll roared. Mickle had just hobbled up. "This whelp o' mine is bargin' me," she told her husband.

"Puh-puh-puh-puh!" said Mickle.

"Only you have a grandchild o' mine in your belly," Poll-Poll told Breda, "I wouldn't bother to advise you. We're campin' down the road an' across the borderline. Come on with us. Let that fellah stay here if he wishes. You're in jeopardy."

Breda looked at Martin. Martin turned away.

"Likely you'll never see Kerry if you stay," Poll-Poll said.

Drawing her shawl higher on her shoulders, Breda came to her feet. She looked uproad into Northern Ireland. The wind soughed in the valley. As a cloud overcast the moon, the lamplight gained in power. "We won't be long breakin' camp," she said quietly to Martin.

"I'll help lift the cart across the barrier," Mickle said.

Martin sat on a stone. He set his lower jaw sideways and balanced tooth on tooth.

"I'm stayin' here!" he said.

"I'll go myself," Breda said.

She made the superfluous preparations of searching for something she had left on the grass margin. "I'm goin'— d'you hear?"

"If you go, you'll never sit on my cart again."

"You're sayin' that to frighten me?"

"I'll put it on me soul!"

"Pay no heed to him," Poll-Poll said. "If he leaves you, our mare is as fast as his cob."

"That oul' mare is liable to drop like a stone," Martin said. "That cart will fall to pieces with woodworm." Directly, to Breda, "Why aren't you goin'?"

Breda looked around her, wildly.

"Come on!" from Poll-Poll.

As the old woman laid her hand on Breda's forearm, "Take your paws off me!" the girl shouted.

"We're tryin' to help you," Mickle said.

"Go 'way, let ye!" Breda yelled.

Poll-Poll flounced heavily away. "Stay, let you! An' if you get a bullet in the—"

"Hike off!" Martin shouted.

"Fry in your grease!" Poll-Poll said.

As the old pair stomped towards the barrier, they were halted by a curlew call.

"What's that?" Poll-Poll asked.

The others did not answer. Again came the double cry of liquid loneliness.

"A curlew screechin'," Mickle said in a tone that conveyed his disbelief. To Martin and Breda, "If ye hear disturbance in the night, close your ears to it." To Poll-Poll, "Hurry, you ape!"

Gripping her skirts at the sides, Poll-Poll squeezed through the barricade in the wake of her husband.

(6)

From where he squatted on the straw spread on the floor, his back against the whitewashed cottage wall, the Peter the Painter within reach of his hand, Frank Horan glanced around at his sprawled companions.

"My third—my secret life—is here," he told himself.

Light from the oil lamp hanging on the kitchen wall fell through the bedroom doorway. Down there, others were dozing or asleep. From the room at the back of the fireplace came the noise of a man snoring.

Frank took up a length of straw, bit it off below a nodule, and began to poke the end of it between his teeth. He took the straw from his mouth and smelled it: he had once seen a dentist do something like this to find if there was a food trap in a patient's mouth. Recalling what he was doing, he threw the straw away.

Removing his spectacles, he cleaned the lenses. With a gesture that had something bookish to it, he replaced the glasses on his nose.

There were perhaps twenty-five men in the cottage. Some were armed with Parabellum and Sten guns. Others had Lee Enfield rifles; a few had shotguns.

All wore tri-coloured arm flashes: this as a sop to international convention on the wearing of uniform and the consequent claiming of prisoner-of-war treatment. On a shovel on the hearthstone lay a number of corks ready for charring over the peat fire. Frank thought this face blackening a messy business; he had even told Lanigan so.

If one got away after the job was over, one couldn't hope to wash the stuff completely off. So that, like a grubby urchin in school, the washline on the neck or wrists would show.

One of the men in the kitchen had begun to tell a story.

The owner of the cottage, a huge, rugged man, leaned forward in his chair and cupped an ear with his hand the better to hear the tale. Now and again, he threw himself against the back of the chair with a bellow of laughter.

"This uncle of mine," the storyteller went on, "was a great man for the beer. Recovering from a bout of booze he'd head for the chapel, a fishin' rod on his shoulder and a line and minnow trailin' behind him. On the Square in front of the chapel he'd start fishin' as if the road was alive with trout. Next he'd prop the rod against the chapel wall and stagger into the house of God.

"Up the sanctuary gate he'd go and light every candle in the candelabrum. But he wouldn't put a ha'penny into the collection box.

"He'd then fill his pockets with pamphlets from the rack—'Sobriety and You,' 'How to Guard the Virtue of Purity,' and 'It Began with Holding Hands.' Finally, he'd abuse Pontius Pilate, the Roman Soldiers, and the Jews in the Stations of the Cross. Home with him then, trailin' his rod behind him.

"The followin' day, when he was sober, the parish priest would take him by the arm and say: 'Candles so much, pamphlets so much, disedifying remarks so much, forbearance on the part of the parish priest so much—a total of three pounds four and tenpence. Pay up, Mick, or I'll change you into a goat.'

"Himself and me uncle'd laugh heartily. Then me uncle would say, 'Bless you, Father, what Pope have we now?' And finally he'd pay up."

Frank looked up at Lanigan. Lanigan glanced at his watch, then came to his feet.

The lamp was lowered. Lanigan tried to pull open the front door; the door was stuck. "We mostly use the back door," the owner of the cottage said. A draught of cool night air entered as the door came abuptly open. The flame in the oil lamp crouched and almost went out; with a belch of smoke rising from the lamp chimney, the flame rose. Lanigan went out, drawing the door to behind him and keeping it barely open with his fingers.

After a time, "Leo!" he called into the kitchen.

The owner of the house waddled to the door. Both men stood on the threshold. Frank could hear their conversation.

"Is that where the road is spiked?" Lanigan asked.

"Aye!"

"Is it a house?"

"No house there."

"Are you sure?"

"I'm sure."

"What is it, so?"

"Could be tinkers."

"Do they generally camp there?"

"I've never seen 'em in that place before. Where the other fire is on our side of the border—those are tinkers for sure."

"That light at the barrier seems bright."

"It's a Tilley lamp above a fire."

From the deep valley came the whistle imitating the cry of a curlew. "The tinkers'll have to take their chance," Lanigan said.

"Och, aye!"

71

Both men returned to the kitchen. Lanigan looked at his watch and signed to a man to put the shovel on the fire.

Is this my true life? Frank asked himself as, through clean lenses, he looked up into Lanigan's face.

Parachute trooper who had come down in Arnheim and had knifed his way out of it, now an anthracite miner in Leitrim, for what he called "cabbage-patch scrapping" on the border between Northern Ireland and the Republic Lanigan had contempt. "You're at this jackin' border for the past forty-five years," he had said, when all were gathered into the cottage, "and you've yet to capture a barracks!"

The fact that this was Lanigan's first time in charge made it more dangerous than usual, Frank thought. The man would possibly attempt something foolhardy to prove himself.

Lanigan glanced sharply in his direction. Frank looked towards the corner of the kitchen: a butterbox of concrete encased in an old snuff tin of scrap iron and gelignite. Come to consider it, it was a footling business. Trying to blow even the remnants of an Empire to pieces with a landmine of cement and snuff tins was ridiculous.

"Okay!" Lanigan said.

The men took berets out of their pockets and drew them on. A fat man wearing a beret too small for him looked idiotic. The men snatched at the charred corks and began to dab their faces. Frank thought that the glee around him had neurotic undertones. "Where's *our* goddam curlew?" Lanigan asked abruptly. "Here!" said a hatchet-faced fellow; licking his lips, he mocked the curlew's call.

All the men were now gathered into the kitchen. "Excuse me!" a man wearing gloves said. "If you're taken, what will you say?" The men murmured incoherently. "Repeat it!"

"For cryin' . . ."

"Please repeat it. It's important."

" 'As soldiers of the Irish Republic, we dispute the right of a foreign power to hold one square foot of Ireland,' " the men said in a shamefaced chant. For a moment there was silence.

Someone put out his tongue through blubbery lips. "Birrp!" he noised in disbelief. All laughed in relief.

Lanigan stood in the doorway. "Keep behind me as we go," he said.

(7)

Mickle still kept his arms extended as if to protect the young pair from the fury of the approaching rival gangs.

"Children walkin' in the dark!" he shouted.

Martin seemed defiantly amused. Breda hid her pale face behind his shoulder. Glancing uproad, she saw Winifred McQueen, and experienced a stab of jealousy.

His right hand trailing an ash crop, Breda's uncle came forward. With a jab of his arm, he sent Mickle sprawling.

Feinting with his right hand, he gripped Breda by the hair with his left. The girl gave a squeal of fear; Martin made no effort to defend her. Her uncle jerked the girl's face close up to his, stripped his teeth and then, tightening his grip on her hair, spun her in the direction of the fire he had just left.

"One stockin' for two legs when you're with Claffeys," he said.

Martin laughed indulgently. Out of an eye corner he saw a half-brother of his secretly holding the kettle bar.

Breda's uncle swilled in his gums, then spat into Martin's face.

Martin gave a shout of laughter. Kettle bar raised above his head, his stepbrother came rushing. The screaming of the women laced the roars of the men.

"Stall your fightin'! We've talked," Martin shouted.

The man with the kettle bar stopped.

"Ye've talked?" he asked.

"We've talked—the *lack* an' myself. We're out to marry."

The tinkers glanced sheepishly at one another. Some tapped the road with the knobs of their sticks. The women mewed with delight.

Mickle was on his feet at once. "Yehoo!" he cried. " 'Tis the will o' God that the Gilligans an' Claffeys should join."

He looked uproad at the knot of McQueens. "Together, we'll whip the world," he called out.

Both clans together jeered at the McQueens.

Moving up the steps to her own caravan, Winifred slammed the brass-mounted door behind her.

Breda's uncle slung the ash crop into the field. Taking Martin by the arm, "Turn your face," he said.

His fingers tautening his sleeve in his palm, he wiped the spittle off Martin's face. Then he banged both his palms together. "Now I could fight the King-Devil!" he said. The tinkers laughed in relief.

Breda looked into her aunt's face. The tired, tawny face

of the oldish woman creased into the semblance of a smile.

"We'll fix this match fair," Mickle went on. "Then I'll manage a weddin' that'll be remembered for ever."

On all sides there rose a gabble of delight.

The tinkers gathered about the Gilligan fire. They brawled and yelled uproariously.

When a child almost fell into the flames, its mother's scream was perfunctory. Mickle's hands flailed in an effort to restore order. Those nearest him he beat with his hat. Breda was resting with her back against the fence. Martin, his arms folded, stood opposite her on the road.

Silence fell on the encampment.

"They'll need a start," Mickle said.

"So they will," the crowd clamoured. A sexual joke convulsed all; Mickle had to begin again.

"What'll ye give the girl?" a Claffey man asked Joe Gilligan.

"What she needs!"

"She'll need a cob—the one ye call Tomboy."

"To fit *your* makin's of a flat cart."

"An' to wear *your* set o' harness."

"Brightened by the silver mountin's you found in the shootin' lodge."

"Give 'em a feather tick!" a wit roared. The women leaned back laughing.

"Ye can't let 'em go empty-handed," Mickle protested.

"Who says we can't?" both principals retorted.

For hours they argued, shouted, cajoled, defied, inveigled, threatened, capitulated, attacked, screeched, and raised such a din as led passers-by to believe that the two bands were about to kill each other.

Time and again, in mid-argument, one of the men burst from the fireside, clumped thirty or forty yards up the road and, whilst micturating, yelled back point after point to buttress his argument. Adjusting his trousers flap with a boylike anger and innocence, he clumped back to the others.

Several times the match seemed broken; at such times Breda glanced up to seek reassurance from Martin. His eyes barely brushed hers, as if considering reassurance unworthy of him. At last, agreement was reached and clenched by the spitting on hands and the slamming of palm on palm.

Mickle rose to his feet. "Good work!" he said. "Ye'll be able to travel in one another's country now." He took out a red handkerchief and pretended to wipe tears from his eyes.

The voice of the wit was heard: "What about the weddin' that'll live for ever in the memory o' man?"

"When a man is fixin' disagreements," Mickle said, "he says many things."

"We'll give you ten minutes to tell us your plan," Breda's uncle said.

"If you fail, we'll pelt you out of the camp," said one of the Claffeys.

Mickle's eyes darted here and there in an effort to find an ally. "I'll go up the road," he said at last, "an' put on my considerin' cap."

"Don't go too far!"

Mickle moved up the road. Now and again he glanced back at the campfires behind him. "I'm God's greatest fool," he told himself as he reached the trees.

(8)

Whispering: "Who is it?"

"Wait!"

"Who the hell is it?"

"It's the second bunch of tinkers."

"Keep behind!"

As Lanigan went quickly along the road edge, Frank Horan was close behind him. With them were two others; beside the road barrier all four men stopped. They stood in the darkness and watched the young pair sitting in the lamplight beside the fire.

Frank indicated to the others that he thought the tinkers were aware of their presence.

The others nodded: the tinker couple were far too innocent-limp, their eyes too fixed on the fire.

Lanigan signed that he was moving forward. He nodded towards the side of the road opposite to that on which the camp was pitched.

As Lanigan moved through the barrier, Breda's back came away from Martin's knee. She pegged a strand of her hair back over one ear.

Lanigan took a few steps forward, then stopped. He looked upwards.

In the sky hung a cloud with a mouth-shaped opening into which the moon was disappearing. When the moon had been swallowed up, Lanigan again moved on; he kept one eye on the tinkers and the other on the road before him. A very young couple, he noted—somewhat garish in dress for the North. Odd, too, they hadn't a dog to give warning.

77

The others were almost past when again the curlew call came—this time from the valley below the road.

Martin turned his head to look at the figures slipping by on the other road edge.

As the light of the lamp took the tinker's face, Frank Horan stopped and allowed the others to pass him by. The young tinker man appeared to be looking straight into his eyes. The girl, too—her eyes were dilated.

"Wha—what time is it?" Breda asked.

With a start, Frank recognised the pair. What were Claffey and the Gilligan girl doing here in the North?

"What time is it?" Breda tried again.

Frank did not reply.

He was thinking of the day Poll-Poll Claffey had brought the boy to Farranagark schoolhouse to be prepared for First Communion; he also remembered that his schoolmaster-father, so impartial that he was partial, had seated the sullen tinker lad beside him in the dual desk.

"Sit down there beside my son Frank"—that's what the old man invariably said when young tinkers or the children of travelling showmen presented themselves for schooling.

Frank clearly recalled that the new scholar's eyes, though brown in colour, were glossed by the blue one sees in the eyes of an unbroken pony. He wore an oversize jacket. Around his throat was a ragged scarf tied with a peculiar knot. He spoke little: like the other boys he got off scraps of religious knowledge by rote: *"Jesus, taking the bread in His Sacred Hands and, raising His eyes to heaven, gave thanks to God the Father . . ."* This young Claffey recited in a singsong voice.

"Ssst!" from Lanigan.

78

Altering his voice, Frank said quietly to the tinkers: "Get into your camp. And stay there!"

Breda and Martin did not reply. Breda glanced up at the lamp. "Leave the lamp alone," Frank added.

"We're goin' to bed, sir," Breda said. The "sir" carried a tonal qualification. Frank moved off to where Lanigan waited.

"Why did you speak to them?" Lanigan whispered angrily.

"I know them."

"I don't give a damn; you shouldn't have spoken to them."

The four men tiptoed on.

As they crossed a field, Frank did not now feel as isolated as before. There was now a link with home. So, as they climbed the fence and moved deeper into the valley, he found himself turning to look back at the lamp hanging from the tree branch.

(9)

Constable Kenneth Yeoman of the Royal Ulster Constabulary lay on an iron bed in an upper room of the barracks. His eyes were fixed on the ceiling.

Now and again he turned his head to glance at the space of dim night sky above the sandbags that covered the lower half of the window.

Early-morning patrols had been common of late, so he had come to bed early. Still he could not sleep. He was thinking of the problem of his courtship.

After a time he swung onto one side and groped on the floor for cigarettes and matches. A cigarette between his lips, he cupped his hand about the matchbox and made the least possible noise when striking the match—this so as not to wake Stewart, who slept in the adjoining bed, or Hamilton, who lay stretched fully dressed on a couch in the corner.

He inhaled deeply, almost gratefully, then sent a smoke ring up into the semidarkness. Whenever he blew a smoke ring at Tuppence, the barracks terrier, the dog backed away, showing its teeth and snapping viciously just short of the breaking smoke ring.

The girl, Patsy Hegarty, a farmer's daughter, lived over the Border in the Republic. Yeoman's lips writhed about the cigarette end as he recalled how the barracks charwoman had once described such a girl: "A polished, picked and painted Papist, a sworn Roman and a true Fenian."

The constable drew deeply on the cigarette; this girl represented everything his family opposed. And yet it seemed to him that, in the unpredictable chemistry of mind and body, the girl and himself fitted each other well.

While she was in his arms the Orange drummers, their wrists bloodied from beating out a tattoo of discord, or the shut faces of the Catholics as they watched a display of that force that was a steel-shod heel above them—both seemed powerless.

He had always dressed in mufti when he moved south to meet her. Their meetings had been by night. Twice she had come across the Border to meet him; they had gone together to a cinema in Belfast.

The sense of latent antagonism made the courtship sweeter. He had thought that their relationship was a secret; but a letter he had received from her that morning (the envelope was addressed to a friendly publican in a nearby border village) told him that the word "Traitor!' had been daubed in whitewash on her father's wall.

The countryside is talking, she had written.

In the next bed Stewart stirred in sleep, grumbled, then rolled heavily off his back. Hamilton had the gift of falling quickly asleep and of sleeping accurately; when he awoke it was with a clean break into wakefulness.

Yeoman blew another smoke ring into the air. How long would it take him to reach a decision? As long as it took to smoke two or three cigarettes?

"You see, Kenneth . . ." she had begun when last he met her.

"What do I see?"

They were in an alcove where the parapet of a one-arched bridge had curved to meet a hedge.

"If we go closer to each other, there will be a hard road back."

In the meadow beyond the fence a corncrake noised.

Then, as now, Yeoman had lighted a cigarette and had begun to blow smoke rings. "Go on!" he said.

"I told the priest about us."

"In confession?"

"Yes."

"Good Lord!"

"I had to ask for advice."

A perfect smoke ring; then he thought: The University of the Paperback had educated the world, all except the Southern Irish. Say what one liked about them, before marriage ninety-five percent of their young women were virgins. That was a comfort for a man who couldn't bear to consider it otherwise.

"The priest said that at my age—twenty-two—he would not favour a mixed marriage. Neither, he felt, would the

81

bishop sanction it. If I was in my late thirties and could show that it was my last chance, there would be some hope. But not now . . ."

I came close to laughing into her face, Kenneth Yeoman remembered. It was hard to imagine this warm-bodied girl on her knees in a confession box, a smell of incense and tallow in the air, whispering through a grille—about me!

"Yes?" he had said aloud.

"We'll fall if we go on. I want to have it settled at once."

"What do you suggest?"

"You could take instruction."

"To become a Pap . . . a Roman?"

The girl nodded.

With a flick of his middle finger he had sent his half-smoked cigarette wheeling through the air to the stream below. "No!" he said, sharply.

For a time the girl said nothing. She stood motionless—her forearms on the parapet of the bridge. Was it possible, Yeoman asked himself, that old men in a far-off city could place a barrier between them?

"What's the alternative?" he asked at last.

"If I marry you, you'll have to agree to something."

"To what?"

"To our children being brought up as Catholics."

He knew that, to her, his laughter sounded like the braying of an ass.

In mid-laughter, "Let's go!" she had said, coldly. They had walked away in silence.

Now everything was snarled up. Yet he couldn't leave matters this way. He had to decide to do something—quickly. He could write to her and say: *Let's both get out of this tight island—Canada, Australia, New Zealand, or the Falklands—I don't care where we go as long as we're to-gether. The years will bring changes. The time will yet come when couples like us won't be a peepshow. I'll tell you what, Patsy; we'll halve the kids. I'll give you the first . . . if there ever is a first. What do you say?*

Too flippant? No harm in trying, Yeoman told himself. I'll get that letter off first thing in the morning. Better get it done while the Border is quiet. I'll tap out the address on the barracks typewriter: don't want the Fenian post-men on the other side to smell a rat. I'll write: *Be at Tom-lin's End next Wednesday night at the usual time: we'll find a way out of this. I'm genuinely sorry for my rudeness.*

The constable drew fully on the cigarette. In the yard of the barracks Tuppence had begun to bark. The terrier, too, was beginning to have the jitters. Mmmh, draw, take smoke deep in, down and hold. Peho-o-o-o-o, up into the opaque overhead, up, up, up . . . a smoke ring for Tuppence the terrier.

(10)

After the four men had passed on, Martin and Breda did not speak.

Breda's eyes strayed to the barricade. Martin, his fingers clamped on his knees, kept his eyes fixed on the fire. Breda's face was pale; her hair, drawn to a knot at the nape of her neck, stressed the line of her profile. The wrist of her right hand was on her knee; her left hand hung dead onto her shin. The wind had begun to complain.

"He said to go into the camp," Breda said at last.

Martin did not move.

After a time, "You're not mad with me?" she asked softly.

"I'm not."

"These days I'm in dread of my shadda. If I should torment you too much, belt me."

Martin nodded gravely.

"One thing only. Keep to my head and neck—that way *he*'ll come to no harm."

"I'll do that."

"A man could belt a woman, an' she'd still be fond of him. You might think, the way I carry on, that I'm not fond of you. That's not true. You're the hill that fills my world. I never got a chance to tell you this before. Often when a woman carries on like I've been doin', she's only testin' her man. Now that I'm quiet, I can see it plain."

She did not speak for a while.

"The puzzle of man an' woman came to my mind again," she went on. "Everythin' about them is queer an' lovely too. I want to be wanted in the crooked way of a woman. The strength of your wantin' is the strength of my fondness for you."

Breda smiled quietly.

Above them the wind played its music.

As if speaking to herself, Breda went on: "Together a man an' woman are like two pieces of a spud that a person'd break in his hands. If the two pieces were put together again, you'd think the spud was never broken. That's the way man fits woman."

Martin gave no indication that he had heard.

"When the priest spoke about us bein' one flesh, I didn't understand. What he meant was that between me an' you there's no shame. For shame has to do only with a second person. An' with the one that is us, there can be no such thing as shame."

Breda sighed. Then, later: "I know you find it hard to

have to go in a straight line through Ireland for four days on end. But already we've one day down an' we won't feel the rest of the road."

She rose from the stone and squatted at his feet, her back against his knees.

"There, now!" she said.

They were at ease for a time. Suddenly, Breda looked up. "What's troublin' you?" she asked.

"Nothin'."

"There *is* somethin'. Tell it to me."

"It's about *him*."

"What about him?"

"When you have him, you won't be bothered with me."

Breda broke into laughter. "You're a grand eedjit of a man," she said.

As Martin made to rise to his feet, she held him by pressing her back against his knees. "That's the nicest thing you ever said to me," she said.

Later: "The fella who spoke . . ." Breda said. Martin raised his head to listen.

"He's from Kerry, the same as us." Suddenly Breda stood up, walked a few restless steps, and said, "I'm sorry we didn't take Poll-Poll's advice."

"Are you still in dread?"

"A little." She moved away a few steps. "Grip me, Martin!" she said.

Martin came to his feet, moved from behind her, and placed his arms around her. "Grip me firmer," she said, "and tighten your hands about me here." She thrust her head backwards against his breast and rocked her head from side to side. Her hands crept around, one on each side, and tightened on the ends of his jacket. She shuddered. "The dread will pass," she said presently. "When we're lyin' face to face in the camp, we'll be all right—the three of us."

He did not answer.

"I have a plan," she said. Her eyes were closed.

"Keep your arms about me," she said, "an' start to sing. Just loud enough for me to hear. In the middle of your song dance me down into the camp. Let it be a song of love."

Again her head lolled against his breast.

Martin began to sing in a low voice:

"No more I'll hear your voice of song in the dewy milking bawn
With the kine all lowin' round you in the faint red light of dawn.
Some other maid will sing those songs while you are in the clay,
O Blessed God! my heart will break for Mary from Loch Ray."

Breda moaned with pleasure.

His lips moving in song, Martin began to move his wife forward and downward into the camp.

With a sigh of pleasure, Breda stretched full length on the straw. Martin continued to hum for a while. Then, slowly, he drew his arms from about her.

For a while he remained looking at the girl's face. Then, still on his haunches, he withdrew. At the mouth of the camp he rested on his right knee and looked up at the sky.

A cloud like a misshapen tower had reared upwards. Its upper edges were blurred by the gold of the hidden moon. The cloud continued to crest higher; then it looked less like a tower than a huge thickset animal straining upwards to reach some prey. Its size made it a yardstick by which Martin could measure the height and breadth of the heavens.

Below it, other clouds, left overlong at the mercy of the weather, pulsed towards the north, but the huge animal cloud seemed bent on reaching upwards into the zenith of the night.

When its shape most closely represented a recognisable animal, such as a bear or a gorilla, it changed and was seen exactly to resemble a dirigible; there was also conveyed an impression of the dirigible being propelled by strong but noiseless engines.

As the cloud continued to scale the sky, the valley below the road, by contrast, became dwarfed: it was now a pit in a groin of the world where only a few lemon-coloured cottage lamps offered solace.

And, with the dwarfing of the valley, the encampment, suspended between height and depth, between zenith and nadir, seemed to dwindle until it was little more than a cigarette spark in grass. So that, at last, the centre of the towering and cowering world was the lamp and, beneath it, the scarlet-white-black ring of the dying fire.

A last turning-over faggot flame took Martin's face.

The wind sobbed once and was still.

As Martin came slowly to his feet, the lamplight began to fail. He was almost erect when Breda asked, sleepily, "The bird's cry—it was false?"

"Aye."

"Would it be smugglers or th' other lads?"

"The other lads," Martin said.

Again the barracks terrier began to bark. Yeoman rolled out of bed.

He took up his Sten gun and went towards the window. He stood looking out over the sandbag barrier. He saw the shape of the hill to the south, with, halfway up its flank, the spark that was the tinkers' lamp. The moonlight was erratic. Very faintly he heard the sound of a vehicle to the north—probably a tender on patrol.

"What is it?" Stewart asked.

As Yeoman turned to answer, the building bucked and made as if to leap upwards. The eardrums took the full force of the explosion. The bedroom door was slammed against the wall. Plaster from the ceiling crashed down beside Hamilton's bed.

The force of the blast flung Yeoman against a dressing table; recovering, he groped through the doorway to the landing. There was a smell of explosive; a cloud of mortar powder rose from the stairwell. Rubble was everywhere underfoot.

The floors of the rooms above him were resonant with the rumble of men groping for their weapons. As Yeoman crunched cautiously down a few steps of the stairway, the air stung his nostrils. At a point in the stairway where he felt he was protected by the sandbag rampart outside the door, he saw that the dayroom door had slewed outwards and was hanging on one hinge. The constable bent down so that he could see into the dayroom. A hole gaped in the gable. He heard the sound of a whistle coming from outside the building.

There was a sense of gathering before jumping.

Then Yeoman saw what he took to be a form leaping through the hole to crouch beside the chimney breast. Poking his weapon between two balusters, he fired; the figure went down. As it tried to rise, Yeoman gave it another burst. The second burst of fire appeared to have no effect on the vague shape; it then rose, took a few steps, stood for a moment or two as if unharmed, and crashed to the floor beside the hole in the wall.

A second figure showed against the lighter background of the night; urgently it called a name.

This time Yeoman aimed at a point lower in the figure. There was a choked exclamation, and the dim outline vanished. The attack on the building was now general.

Outside, the noise of the vehicles grew louder. Yeoman was conscious of no great excitement: he had a sense of having rehearsed this action so often that the reality came as an anticlimax. The stairs resounded with pounding boots as men rushed past him to take up posts in the rooms on the ground floor. He held his position on the stairs.

Yeoman was aware of a seepage of sadness—not for the man who lay prone below him, but for himself. These things could not be hidden from a woman. Blood is between the Papists and my people, he told himself: the senseless blood that is now dribbling on to rubble on the dayroom floor.

He felt a sense of relief; for the moment, his personal problem seemed solved. He began to fire sporadically through the hole in the gable.

Lying in the camp, Martin, too, had listened to the terrier barking.

"I'm sleepy," Breda murmured almost inaudibly.

Martin drew the shawl around his wife's shoulders.

It was warm in the tent. The smell of burnt faggot pervaded the confined space.

He waited until her breathing had settled. Then he moved quietly out of the camp. He glanced upwards; the lamp was almost out.

He walked downroad in the direction taken by the four men. At every sound he stood still, listened, and looked about him. He came to a gap in the hedge; here he placed one forearm on the fence and, leaning forward, looked across the ravine. From the fields beneath him came the smell of old hay. A smudge in a corner of the meadow—that was Tomboy. The windrows were cream-coloured in the moonlight. The valley looked harmless. In the sky the moon floated in an area defined by ragged cloud edges.

The remembered voice of the stranger continued to tantalize him; yet the man's name eluded him. He kept thinking that the travelling man who forgets a voice is a fool.

He heard the drone of vehicles coming from the north. He saw the lights of the leading vehicle and sensed power in the noise of its engine. At some distance behind it, other vehicles strained. The terrier's barking took on a note of frenzy.

As Martin gave a final look down into the valley, there was an explosion so violent that it made a weapon of the air and slammed it twice against his head.

Then a whistle pealed. There came the sound of what appeared to be hammer blows on planks. The area to the northeast was ragged with flashes. Martin raced for the camp.

Throwing himself at the mouth of the tent, he crashed into Breda coming out. He fell awkwardly on his side to the straw. "Jesus!" Breda yell-moaned, sprawling outwards so that she almost pitched on top of the embers. Wrenching her body, she came to her feet.

Below her the valley was loud with the stutter-stammer of automatic fire.

"Poll-Poll!" Breda screamed as she ran towards the barrier.

Martin raced after her and caught her. She broke away and fell to the roadway. As he tried to raise her, she clawed at his face. "Jesus of Calvary!" she yelled and, again, "Poll-Poll!"

The sound of the firing reached a crescendo. Martin shouted into his wife's face. He had to use all his strength to drag her backwards; with a heave he sent her into the camp. Holding her down with one hand, he groped for the canvas flaps. As these fell into place, he pitched full length close to his wife. Her panting was that of a spent dog. After a time the firing became desultory. A whistle blast, first fruitless in its seeming effort to stop the firing; as again it began to blow insistently the firing ceased, except for a desultory shot here and there in the fields.

The whine of the tender came insistently. After a burst of automatic fire the curlew call was heard; in it was implicit the sadness of a bird lost in misted air.

Then came the howling of hounds.

(12)

To Frank Horan it was as if a series of jabs from a riveting tool had hammered across his thighs. He was aware of blood leakage, but it didn't seem notable; he recalled the sensation of experiencing sudden power and sudden release.

He was beside Lanigan as the miner had jumped over

the rubble into the dayroom; what the other proposed doing once he was in the building Frank did not know. There was a vague idea of "blowing them to hell out of it." He had been peering across the tumbled bricks and stone of the breach when Lanigan had been pumped into: once, pause, twice, pause, up, down, caput.

Frank, with a crazy idea of dragging Lanigan out, had got on to the rubble; after this he remembered the gunfire working on him in a horizontal line halfway between his kneecaps and genitals.

As he stumbled back and out, his glasses had fallen off. In his nostrils was the smell he associated with Dodgem cars on carnival days in southern villages. One of the others caught him by the tail of his jacket and flung him sprawling against the gable. He managed to hold his feet. From the roadway above, the tender began to open fire on them. Frank realized that he and two others were cornered in the angle between the roadway and the barracks. He still clutched his gun.

The fingers on his left hand had begun plucking the clinging cloth of his trousers legs out from his thighs. He could barely discern sky from land. He began to vomit the sandwiches he had eaten in the cottage kitchen; a shape moved aside to avoid his spewing mouth. "You hit?" the shape asked. "My glasses," Frank said, his fingers still plucking. "What are yeh saying?" the shape shouted above the noise of the firing. "It's my glasses!" Frank said.

He tried to grope on the ground, but the form pushed him to one side. "Get goin' or I'll give yeh the boot!" a voice said.

The hill was there—There? He remembered a wall, and found it. He began to blunder-stagger along it. The din was now no concern of his: he was outside it. The wall fell into nothingness. Perhaps he could move more accurately with his eyes closed; no, the exposed eyeballs helped somehow. He was conscious of trudging across a field, of slithering down a declivity.

A brain compass told him that somewhere up there, beyond the tinkers' lamp, was the Border. The declivity grew steep, then sheer; he tumbled into water and lay in it luxuriantly. Clutching at grass, he fought up. Then he heard the hounds.

The whistles began as he climbed the scrub on the other side of the stream. Across-the-border spelled sea and sunlight, the harnessmaker's shop at night, the ping-pong table of a small town; this side spelled rope or years in a latrine-smelling cell.

He was now on a level with the main area of firing across the ravine.

He fell in midfield. He opposed himself to the idea of lying there listening to the tracker dogs. It was so like the music of the beagles crying from Glenoe up into Filemore and away the lope of twenty miles into the Reeks, the pack swinging in a scythe of fury. From the back of Dunkerron Hospital he could see them come pelting down, keeping accurately on the trail of the dog-fox. Again his fingers began plucking; he must be close to being leaked dry.

Lines from a poem came to him:

From their shadowy cotes, the white breasts peep
Of doves, in a silver-feathered sleep . . .

On his knees now. If he didn't get up, the vehicles would beat him to the border. *From their shadowy bloody cotes, the god-forsaken white breasts peeped.* Blind as the proverbial bat, he told himself, I am mendicant to light and shade. The cry of hounds was a magic carpet of memory: Go on, Finder! Go on, Joker! Go on, Judy! Good girl, Judy, find and kill!

In a film tearing in biassed projection, he again saw Lanigan buckle and pitch. He heard the knocking of a coin on glass and a piping voice ask for cascara segrada.

Scattered! *In the year ninety-eight when our troubles were great, and the boys were all scattered and battered and bate* . . . Good tawny moon! Hide your apish face. *This way and that she peers, and sees silver fruit upon silver trees.* Up, Frank Horan, up! 'At's the boy! forget the baying behind you. . . . *Catch her strumpets of beams beneath the silvery degrading thatch.* Above you is Claffey, and above him again your fool father; his face idiotic with the love of scholarship, he the archetypal schoolmaster of the hills, complete with stiff-winged shirtfront and sliding Adam's apple, his hand on Claffey's shoulder as the tinker boy knelt before the bishop to be confirmed . . . *oil of olives mixed with balm and blessed by the bishop on Holy Thursday* . . .

Horan, purblind pestle-pounder, you are at last standing on your drained legs. *And moveless fish in the water gleam* . . . Steady, O affectionate heaving ground . . . Remembering: to the beagle the smell of fox is as the smell of cigar smoke to a human. Remembering: the blood coition experienced on hearing them give open tongue as they hunt in view ("Every night for thirty years as I was filling out beer in an Irish bar in downtown Milwaukee, I heard those doggone beagles cry, so help me God, Frankie boy, I did"). Step after Calvary step. The hounds checked . . . (the frosted air digging into the sinuses). Judy has it! Living Creator! She has a tongue like a Mass bell. . . . She's level with me now (or then?) across the chasm the giant

jumped in the dawn of time. Good girl, Judy. Find him
—me—Judy. Kill him—me—Judy. *Crouched in his kennel
like a log, with paws of silver sleeps the dog* . . . Your father again, his neck no-man's-landed with the acne pits of
ancient adolescence; in the picture book out of the library
box, Karodi the Negro boy looking at the crest of Mount
Kenya, thinking of the elephants pushing through the
bamboo canes . . . that's it, Frankie, a little wine for the
belly's sake . . . making no promises, son, but who knows
but that your diligence may win for you proprietorship of
this Medical Hall . . . Steady . . . whoa, globe! Why
cleave my fork with your monstrous lurching?

Step after splay-legged step, Horan moved upwards.

He threshed down upon the clay fence. After a time he
opened his eyes. Green canvas? Here it is. That burnt-
faggot smell? Right, again. This is it—El Dorado, Journey's
End, caravanserai.

"Tinker!"

Was the silence a trick of his ears? Was there really tur-
moil everywhere? Were peace and hullabaloo pups of one
litter?

"Claffey!"

The hounds were at the water. The tender was check-
ing, seeking, and would soon find. He called on legs of
heated candlewax. He dragged the upper part of his body
higher on the fence and tried to claw at the canvas. He did
not succeed.

He heard his own hoarse voice say: "I'm Frank Horan of
Farranagark . . . outside Kenmare. We sat together . . ."

The baying of the hounds was the slow opening of a red
fan. Semiperipheral eyesight or intuition told him that by
the bridge to the deep left, light had begun to arc-swing.
"If you don't help me across the Border, I'll have you cru-

cified in Kerry"—an illogical threat. Pleadingly, "It's my glasses." With a last effort that even he himself foresaw would collapse in melodrama, "You often filled your belly at my mother's table."

The anger aroused by the tinker's apparent ingratitude gave Horan the strength to draw himself over the fence. He collapsed on the other side.

Head downwards, he found his nose close to the ashes, and his feet hung on the clay bank. His breathing was the snoring of a dog.

Above him then was a blurred outline; he suddenly experienced the smell of charred faggot—and of woman.

"Martin!" Breda called. Martin came out of the tent.

Bent under the weight of the man on his shoulders, Martin staggered towards the barrier. As he and his load became jammed between two spikes, Breda pushed them through. The gun fell from Frank's hand—Breda cried out as it struck her on the instep. After Martin had swayed away, she picked up the weapon and threw it into the deep grass behind the cart. Then she scrambled into the camp.

Beyond the fence, the baying of hounds exploded. A vehicle was heard straining against an incline. For Breda, time was an elastic band drawn taut. As Martin came hurtling to fill the space she had left vacant for him, the camp and its surroundings were drenched in a harsh light.

(13)

The lair of male and female, Kenneth Yeoman thought. He bent and looked into the camp.

He had never before been so close to a tinker's tent; the sense of intimacy it conveyed came to him with something of a shock.

The place exuded the body warmth of a couple compelled by circumstances to live at closest quarters with each other.

At first sight it seemed obscene that man and woman should lie down under such conditions.

A question formed in the constable's mind: Were these the requisite conditions under which man and wife, the conventions and accretions of civilization sloughed, fused and became one in the truest sense of male-female fusion?

The others were coming up. "All right!" Yeoman said to the tinker pair. "Out!"

First Breda, then Martin—their eyes edging away from the light—came out of the camp. Martin had allowed his lower jaw to drop.

A District Inspector of Police asked quietly, "Who are you?"

"Travellin' people," Breda said.

"Where are you from?'

"From the Republic, sir."

"What are you doin' here?"

"Sleepin', sir."

"Do you sleep in your clothes?"

"We do, sir."

"What are your names?"

"He's Martin Claffey. I'm Breda Claffey, his wife."

The Inspector nodded to Yeoman. "See what's inside," he said.

Again, Yeoman went on his hands and knees, and moved just inside the tent. He paused, sniffed deeply, then shuffled forward on the clean straw. Inside the hot half-cylinder of green canvas, he kept up the semblance of searching.

His mind was racing: Here the call of man and woman

for each other seemed more powerful than seas of spilled blood. His girl and himself here and the superfluous world excluded—the concept had a grip on every part of him. His body grew tense with a tenseness he had never before experienced. Then, with a start, he realised that, a short time before, he had, for the first time in his life, killed a man and that the sensation of having killed now seemed trivial. This is something in me that I never thought existed, he told himself; it is as if for the first time I have opened a box inside the box of my deepest emotions.

He was more conscious of life than of death, of love than of hatred, of union than of sundering.

He could have knelt there for a long time finding new perspectives. He backed out of the tent, came to his feet, and said, "Nothing there, sir."

"Seen anyone?" the Inspector asked the tinker couple.

"Expect that scum to tell the truth?" a Sergeant said.

"Has anybody passed this way?" the Inspector again asked.

"The fella you're after—he went that way five minutes ago." Breda indicated the fence at the other side of the road.

"Wouldn't believe a Fenian's oath," the Sergeant said.

"It's God's truth," Breda said in a low voice. "His hand was hangin'—he's gone that way."

She pointed directly across the road. A knot of Special Constables had gathered at the barrier.

"He went across the Border, and you know it!" the Sergeant said. "Did you help him over?"

"As sure as God, we put no hand on him," Breda whined.

"You dumb?" the Inspector asked Martin.

"No," Martin said, with a hoarse gurgle.

"Say 'sir'!" The Sergeant jabbed Martin into the breast with the butt of his rifle, sending him staggering backwards. "Easy!" the District Inspector said.

Snatching at Martin's wrist, the Sergeant held up the tinker's hand. The palm and wrist were blood-smeared. Breda thrust forward. "As we were crawling out of the camp," she said, "my man put his hands on the blood here in the grass."

She went on her knees and ran her palms over the grass, then showed her stained palms. "The fella that's gone was bleedin' like a pig," she said. The Sergeant still held Martin's hand. "I'll prove it to ye," Breda gabbled on. "The cowardly bastar' threw down his gun." She began to search behind the cart, found the weapon, held it up awkwardly, and said, "There now, sir, amn't I tellin' truth?" She came to her feet.

The Inspector balanced the weapon on the palm of his hand, "Come along," he said.

"Where?" Breda asked.

"We're taking you in for questioning."

"No!"

Breda moved towards the Inspector and, as if her body were weightless, executed what appeared to be a dance step. "No," she pleaded, "God love ye, sirs, don't delay us. The child is flattened in my womb. I'm on the road to where he'll see the light. We've told the truth."

She whirled in the searchlight, her features now black and white.

"What do we travellers know or care about the goddamn IRA's?" she shouted. "Or if this country is broken into two, or two thousand, bits? Isn't every hand, North an' South lifted against us? Let us go, I beg of ye."

The men at the barrier had turned to listen.

Falling to her knees beside Yeoman, she pressed his hand to her lips. "By the eyes an' mouth of your woman, ask him to let us go." Again she kissed his hand. "By the fingers that'll yet press a woman's body again' yours, I beg you, sir, ask the big man to tell us go."

Yeoman looked embarrassedly at the Inspector.

East in the ravine, firing broke out. The District Inspector turned, then gestured towards the vehicles. "On your way!" he said, wearily.

As the party of constables went away, Yeoman gave a last look backwards at the tent. He raised his hand to his nostrils and smelled at it. The light swung away, and the men were lost in the darkness.

After they had gone, Martin and Breda remained seated in the camp. They did not speak. They listened as the sporadic firing moved away to the east, where at last it ceased. At last they heard a faint noise from the road barrier.

"Psst!"

"It's Mickle!" Breda whispered.

"Are they gone?" Mickle croaked.

To Martin, Breda said: "Quick! Get the cob. We'll pull the camp." She came out of the shelter. To Mickle: "Give us a hand to get outa here."

Mickle came closer to the camp. "I thought they were cross-questionin' ye," he said, "an' I was goin' to . . ."

"In your red rump!" Poll-Poll had just come up. To the others, she said: "A cattle lorry was waitin' for the wounded fella beyond." To Martin, "He spoke your name."

Breda was dragging the canvas off the camp and tugging

the rods out of the clay. "He's Master Horan's son of Farranagark. Martin carried him across the line," she said.

"I own to God!" Mickle exclaimed. "Shiny Pants Horan will stand me many a glass o' whiskey for this."

"Drag the flat to the barrier," Breda spat at Mickle, "an' help hoist it over." To Poll-Poll: "Gather the rods! Don't stand there with your hands hangin'."

Wheezingly, Poll-Poll began to tug at the rods. In the meadow, Martin could be heard softly calling, "Tomboy!"

As if it had been switched on, the moon came up and illuminated everything. Poll-Poll, her arms laden with rods, stopped to look up at it. "Blessed hour," she said, "what a bugger of a moon!"

Clasping the rods tightly to her, she continued to look up. "Seas an' dust, magpies an' rocks, rabbits' meat an' whiskey, roads an' wheels all hung high in the air. There ye are," she told the moon, "full once a month, an' I'm full every night o' the week!"

Her face cracked in delight.

"I'm sixty-eight come Michaelmas," she said, "an' I've put three husbands through my hands. I'll soon be facin' my Maker, yet I wouldn't be surprised with all this tallyho if I dropped a kid myself the minute we reached that bloody Spike."

Tomboy came jogging towards them. Martin was holding the animal by the forelock and urging it forward. Her face again upturned to the lighted sky, Poll-Poll laughed outright.

THREE

There's some believe that stealing is a sin
and no mistake
And there's more begrudge the sunlight to go
shining on a lake,
And if Hunger is a snowman whose timber arm
can strike
The young can bind the belly and the old
can seek a Spike.

Squirming in silver, lake water moved under the eye of the setting sun.

On the eastern shore of the lake were thatched farmhouses with fences of whitethorn about their paddocks. Elsewhere, tufted trees were spaced in the parklands of crumbling mansions.

Beside the lakeshore road and close to a wall matted with ivy, with the tops of apple trees showing above it, the rods of the camp stood upright. The holed ridgepole was on the grass. The small fire had blackened a circle in the grass. On the far shore of the lake, the Clare hills hid head behind head.

For the tinker pair it had been a long haul through the Midlands.

They had been on the road at daybreak; doggedly the cob had kept going, its bells ringing, its harness mountings glittering, its tail tapering almost to the roadway. Somewhere behind them Mickle and Poll-Poll had laboured to keep in touch with them.

Breda was rinsing garments at the lake edge. She had already spread a magpie selection of washed clothes on the bushes. The girl's face showed signs of strain.

This evening she found the *cloppety-clop* of the cob's hooves resounding in her head. This was unusual. Always since childhood, after a day's travelling, she had been able to set the noise aside.

In her mind pictures of what she had seen during the day came and went.

The chill lakes of Cavan selvedged with reeds . . .

The bony pastures of the upper Midlands with the white heads of Hereford cattle everywhere gaping . . .

The blue-green grass of North Tipperary. A gapped mountain that, legend said, the devil had bitten off and spat out . . .

Almost a hundred white-robed nuns standing in a recessed gateway; each bore a lighted candle in her hand, and as a motorcar moved away the nuns sang, "Go ye afar . . ."

Martin drove by the sun. The day had been clear and sunny since early morning. On the main roads he was ill at ease: the hooting of horns, the stares of people through the windows of touring coaches, the *pock-a-pock* of motor cycles and scooters made the cob and its master uneasy. But when, again, the side roads, limestone-dusty, leading to quiet villages, spun from under the wheels, Martin, Breda, and Tomboy were at ease.

About noon the band had fallen off a wheel. Martin took a moment or two to recognise the object bowling behind them for what it was: his face chilled at the realisation that one of the wheels was riding on its sun-dried felloes.

He drew Tomboy to a halt and then fished the rim out of a roadside ditch. Examining the rimless wheel, he decided that it would bear Breda a little further if she sat on the other side of the vehicle. Leading the animal, he continued on his way, stopping now and again to enquire for a wheelwright.

They came to a thatched cottage built below road level. The wheelwright was old; his fingers ran tremblingly over the felloes. "I haven't shod a wheel for two years," he said. Looking at Breda, he added, "I'll shoe this one."

Martin drew the vehicle in by the open space beside a nearby stream where, half covered with grass, lay a flagstone with a round hole in it. Breda came off the vehicle. From a nearby rick of turf, Martin brought sods to make a circular fire to redden the rim.

For a while Breda sat in the shade of elderbushes; then she rose and took a pint bottle from the cart. She walked upwards to the roadway; on the brow of a ridge to the south lay a long farmhouse. In the meadows behind it a mowing machine noised. The air Breda inhaled through her nostrils was heavy with the smell of the newly cut corn.

She noted the air of prosperity that hung about the farmstead; her eyes took in the red barn, the sprawl of outhouses, the electric poles, the orchard, the pigsties, the flock of hens, and the trimmed dungheap set at a discreet distance from the house.

The side wicket by which she entered was painted white, as was the front door of the house. Below the house, riverside fields were pied with Holstein cattle.

Breda went around by the gable and, entering the porch by the back door, stood in the inner open doorway that led to the kitchen.

The farm wife, her face flushed from baking, turned sharply from the range.

The woman was about forty years of age, swarthy, and cleanly dressed. Breda drew her shawl about her in such a way as told its own story.

"What do you want?" the woman asked.

"A drop o' colourin', ma'am." Breda held out the pint bottle.

"I have no milk."

"A small drop for the love o' God's mother!"

The woman snatched a piece of brown paper from the kitchen window. "Take off the cork," she said.

Without touching the bottle, she wrapped it in the paper. She entered the linney off the kitchen and presently reappeared with a jug of milk in her right hand and the wrapped bottle in her left. Keeping a vague watch on Breda, the woman poured the milk; she took care that the lip of the jug did not touch the mouth of the bottle.

As the milk gurgled in, Breda's eyes secretly took in the details of the dresser with its array of old delph. In a bedroom off the kitchen the furniture was of dark mahogany. Glancing at the electric cooker in the corner, Breda wondered why the farm wife did not choose to bake in it instead of in the range.

The woman held out the full bottle, then turned away. Breda pressed the cork home, thrust the bottle under her shawl, and waited.

The woman turned; at the base of her neck a goitre ring showed.

"What are you waiting for?" she asked.

"You're troubled, ma'am?"

"Troubled?"

"It's a pity your body isn't broken by a child."

The woman's nostrils flared. "It *is* a pity!" she blurted. She walked towards the window and looked out on the fields. "I'd give a lot to be the way you are," she said.

"Time enough, lady!"

"Twenty years is too much time!" Passionately: "Is God fair?"

"I found Him fair enough, ma'am."

"Fair! To give you, a tinker girl, what I'd give my right eye to have."

"If a child won't make you laugh, he won't make you cry."

" 'Twas a liar said it!"

"The world is many things."

"To me, it's the one." Then, "What does it feel like?"

"This?"

"Yes."

"It's to be full as this bottle is full. It's to be all nature."

The farm wife came nearer. Breda saw that the pupils of her eyes were dark hazel in colour and were flecked with points of a lighter hue. "You're not from these parts?" the woman asked.

"I'm from the South."

"You'll hardly come this way again?"

"No."

The woman gave a high-pitched laugh. "Everywhere I go, I hear a child crying," she said. "The land will go out of his name."

A button rang on the edge of the range as the woman tore open her blouse. "Spit on your fingertips, girl," she said, "and put them on my teats. Then, in the name of Mary, wish me luck."

The woman's eyelids closed. She stood with her breasts bared.

Breda wet her fingertips in her mouth, then placed them first on one teat, then on the other.

Buttoning her blouse, the woman turned away. She went to the dresser, put her hand into a bowl, and brought out some silver.

Breda was at the door. "Thanks for the milk, ma'am,"

she said, and hurried away. She reached the wheelwright's cottage in time to see the shod wheel roll into the pool and send up a puff of steam.

"Who was in the *keena?*" Martin asked, as they jogged along.

"The *beoir* of a *sham*."

"What did she say?"

"Nothin'!"

"She gave you milk?"

"Aye."

Breda's eyes were on the road before her. "Go on, Tomboy!" Martin said, as the cob showed signs of lagging. He leaned over the side of the cart to see how the newly shod wheel was faring. Again he looked at his wife. She was looking down at the backs of her fingers. Women are forever thinking back, Martin told himself.

(2)

The two clans were glaring uproad into the darkness.

"Mickle!"—it was the raised voice of the wit—"Tell us your plan for the weddin'."

Mickle came hurrying towards the fire. "It broke across my brain," he said.

"Eh?"

"What Dickybird said."

"What did that mad tramp say?'

"That once we were kings."

"Kings?" Both families chorused in laughter.

"And because the foreigners flung us out of our castles," Mickle went on, "we could never find houses fit for us to live in. So we did without houses altogether."

Another burst of laughter.

"He told me, too, that when we had our land, bishops and archbishops were proud to marry our young couples."

Poll-Poll slapped her rump in disdain.

"No laughin'!" Mickle shouted. "Mebbe now . . ."

"Mebbe what?"

"Where we're camped here is near the palace of an Archbishop. What do ye say to my Grace himself spancellin' this pair?"

"Racs-fol-ol-dee-deedle-tay-ri-o!" Poll-Poll chanted as she stamped around the fire.

"Ye doubt me?" Mickle shouted.

"Anyone that married Poll-Poll couldn't be doubted!" from the wit.

Poll-Poll stopped her war dance. "He's the best of the three men I had," she said—then added, impishly, "what's left of him!"

Again the torrent of jeers.

"Leave it to me!" Mickle yelled.

"If you make a mockery of my brother's daughter," Breda's uncle said, "I'll roast you over a fire."

Early next morning, two springcarts left the encampment. Mickle, Poll-Poll, and Martin were in the leading vehicle; in the other were Breda, her uncle, and aunt.

The unshod ponies moved at a quick pace over the stony roads.

Where the road reached the top of the hill, Southwest Ireland was spread below them like a frayed chart. Immediately beneath them in the sheltered valleys were the plumes of foreign trees. Between the estates and the ocean lay lakes, farmhouses, and waterfalls.

The deft ponies trotted downhill by little roads that twisted around mown meadows. The wheels spun past monkey-puzzle trees growing beside pillared doorways, past boats moored in lake bays, until at last through the copper beeches the tinkers saw the cathedral spire.

Breviary in hand, His Grace the Archbishop paced in his garden. In mid-lawn, beyond the rosebeds, was a marble statue of the Virgin and Child.

In the laneway beside the garden, Mickle signalled to those in the other springcart to stop. He then guided his mare forward until the inner cartwheel was close to the old wall.

Standing upright in the vehicle, he gripped the coping of the wall and pulled himself up. His face framed by stalks of valerian, he peeped in. He grunted his satisfaction at what he saw.

Driving the mare off the pathway and onto the roadway, he tied her by the reins to a telegraph pole at the side of the road opposite the footpath. Breda's uncle tied his animal to the setlock of Mickle's cart.

Mickle led the five others to a recessed doorway in the garden wall. He turned the knob and grinned to find the door unlocked. A pathway shaded by privet led forward. Mickle gestured the others to come inside the door and then closed it noiselessly behind them. He spread his fingers in warning.

The boots of the Archbishop, noising in gravel, drew nearer. The tinkers bent their heads. As, silently reciting his Office, the Archbishop reached the end of the pathway, Mickle slid from behind the bushes and, hat in hand, came to a halt before him.

"The blessin' o' God on you, me Grace!"

The Archbishop was a tall man, with high cheekbones that gave his features an Eastern cast.

He looked at the doorway and, seeing the heads of the other tinkers, frowned. He began to fumble in his pocket for some coins.

·"Not that!" Mickle said.

"Hmmh?"

"It's about a marriage, me Grace!"

As Mickle's left hand signalled to the others, Martin and Breda were pushed to the front.

The Archbishop eyed the young pair. "Ask at the presbytery for Father Bergin," he said, then turned to walk away.

Mickle, his arms outstretched as if he were trying to stop a runaway colt, stood before him.

"Me Grace!"

"Yes?"

Mickle gestured towards Martin and Breda.

"You want *me* to marry them?" As Mickle gulped agreement, the Archbishop looked glum. "What parish are you from?" he asked.

"The Parish of Ireland," Mickle said.

"Are you Catholics?"

The tinkers gave a cry of sham insult.

"Is there a priest who knows you well?"

"There is, indeed!" from Mickle.

"Who is he?"

"Father Costello of Honeyground in the County Limerick. But he had a stroke twelve months ago. And there's a Father Melody, a holy father in the city of Dublin."

"Father Melody?"

"Both of them will go bail for us, me Grace."

113

The Archbishop's eyes twinkled. "Why do you want *me* to marry them?"

"Because of what Dickybird said."

"Who is Dickybird?"

"A travellin' man with learnin'."

"What did Dickybird say?"

"He said that long ago we were kings. That we had beggars at our gates. So we think that, for once, this pair shouldn't be tied by a hungry curate."

The Archbishop's eyes moved from one to another of the band confronting him. "Are these two related?" he asked.

"No relation, me Grace."

"What age are you?" the Archbishop asked Breda.

"Touchin' seventeen, Father."

" 'Me Grace!' " Mickle roared.

"Me Grace!"

"Have you been baptised?"

Breda's aunt began to wail: "Her ma an' da are dead, me Lord, but she was christened Breda Hanora Gilligan of a mornin' in May in or around the Fair of the Cross by Father Humphries, God rest him."

To Martin, "What age are you?"

"Gone eighteen, me Grace."

"Were *you* baptised?"

"The market day that young Jack was ruptured by a kick of the geldin' . . ." Poll-Poll began.

The Archbishop beckoned Martin to draw level with the girl. "Join your hands, both of you," he said, "and recite the Lord's Prayer."

"Is it in Irish, English, or our own gammon?" Breda asked with a sudden brightness to her eye.

"English!"

Breda interlaced her fingers. As her eyes stabbed sideways, Martin put his hands together in the shelter of his hat. Together they began to recite the prayer.

On the gravel pathway a thrush breaking a snailshell stopped to listen to the sketchy recital.

When they had finished: "When do you wish to be married?" the Archbishop asked.

"Whatever day you'll name, me Grace," Mickle said.

"Tuesday morning in the cathedral at seven thirty, I'll make enquiries of your . . . mmm! . . . Father Melody."

"You'll wed them yourself?" Mickle asked.

The Archbishop nodded.

Amid a gabble of blessings, the Archbishop turned away and resumed the reading of his breviary.

(3)

Do not move! You hear me, fish?

Wedge lying by the weed at the lake edge, the water making you appear smaller than you are, slender black wedge—whoa! steady! That's the boy! Let there be a slight movement of your tail. No more! Understand? At your service, fish, your obedient servant, Martin Claffey, travellin' man.

Seen from above, salmon, you are black-dark; seen from the side, I know that you are red silver finin' down into white. There you are, lyin' in hide from the sun. I know how things are with you, fish—it's many the summer's day I felt the same way myself, lazin' after joggin' all day in my cart.

You aren't a chunky German salmon nor an old unmated fellah who spent the winter lookin' in vain for a partner. No! you're a bar o' silver fresh-run from the sea. Amn't I the devil's son to come between you an' life? You've earned your time here after your struggle up the Shannon, thinkin' that after you've rested you'll move ahead till you find the water of a side river cool on your gills. An' you'll follow it—if you're allowed!

Don't stir, boyo! . . . that's only an innocent cord I've thrown across your back. All I want to do is to snatch you with a bit of a strokehaul. You wouldn't blame me for that?

Steady now! No fuss! . . . a few steaks of your middle I want—one for myself, one for Breda, one for Poll-Poll, an' one for that sanovabitch, my stepfather. You couldn't refuse us that? If I let you off, an Englishman'll hook you. Would that be fair to Old Ireland?

I'll move a step closer to you, my honey fish, so don't take fright an' run away. After I've laid you out on the grass you'll be a handsome sight in blood an' silver. That cast went right across your back . . . where the flamin' hell is my line? My eyes are blurry from the sun.

Steady footin' is what I need. If I had my boots wedged between the stones I could harness you an' break you.

I bear you no grudge, salmon. Listen to my side of the story: my wife is close to her time an' needs nourishment. Whoa! . . . steady . . . don't take fright. Holy Immortal Creator, I thought you had gone.

Let me explain: that's silver paper dangling as a dropper below the joint of the treble . . . if I don't have that as a marker, I can't see the hooks in the water, an' then you'll get away. That would never do!

So, lie still, girl. . . . I didn't lay a finger on you yet . . . fair play, bonny play, did I? Stay still or I'll get cross with you. That's better.

My mouth fills with spit when I think of your flesh, hot or cold, comin' out in layers of pink. . . . Where the hell did my line go that time?

"Martin! What are you doin'?"

Are women eedjity? She's standin' on the bank, an' I'm up to my thighs in water. An' she asks me what the hell I'm doin'!

A beauty cast. Just right . . . Steady now, Claffey, boy from nowhere, anywhere, and everywhere . . . Let's check everything. The stick? Held steady with spits. The line? Lying across the fish halfway between tip an' tail. The hands? Ready for a low-drawn pull that's certain to strike home.

All correct!

So now, in God's name, all precautions taken, my toes dug in securely between stones, my balance ensured, I'll put my strength into one steady strong . . .

"Martin!"

"What?"

"Don't snatch him yet!"

"Why not?"

"There's someone comin' "

"The curse of the . . ."

"It's a priest."

For a moment, Martin hung loosely above the salmon. Then he dragged his shoes carefully along the stones as he moved to the shore.

(4)

"Silver," Mickle breathed. The old country-man seated on the rope chair glanced up.

Mickle looked cautiously round the cabin interior. His

117

eyes rested for a moment on a picture of Robert Emmet in heroic stance and profile.

Must get working fast, he told himself, if we're to catch up with the others.

He put his hand inside his jacket and took out a bar of solder.

"Silver?" the countryman asked.

Under the peak of his cap, his eyes had come alive. Mickle brought his mouth close to the countryman's ear.

"I make my bivvy in this quarry one night," he said. "I wake to see a fellow hammerin' on the stones of the wall. I shine a match on him. 'What are you doin'?' says I. He got a fright. There it was on the quarry wall—a vein of silver.

"Only a fool sweats blood to live," Mickle said. He handed the solder bar to the countryman.

From inside his scarecrow jacket, the tinker took soiled tissue paper; from this he unwrapped two new half-crowns. "I make them," he said modestly.

The cottier took the coins and, placing one between his lips, bit firmly on it. He lifted the coins to the light and squinted at them. "Hmm!" he said.

Mickle took back the coins. For a moment he let them lie on the palm of his left hand. He spun one up into a ray of sunlight that had shafted through the cabin window. He caught the coin as it fell. "Money for old rope!" he chuckled.

He folded the coins in the paper and replaced them in his inside pocket. He thrust the solder into the outside pocket of his jacket. Stretching his arms, he yawned. "You're poverty-stricken an' old," he told the countryman. "Tonight I'll make forty coins. I'd make more, only they're heavy in the pocket."

Mickle looked out over the half-door. Crouched in the

cart, Poll-Poll was dozing. Now and again her head nodded forward. The mare's head drooped in weariness.

"Ten years ago a certain farmer was a smallholder," Mickle went on. "Now he has the grass o' thirty cows, all of them slow roomy waltzers."

He drew closer to his prey. "He gives me notes to buy the stuff: I do the rest myself. He's disappointed me—he turned out a bloody miser."

Mickle saw the other's jaws working.

"If I could get a fi'-pound note now, I could make fifty pounds' worth of half-crowns. If I could find a close-mouthed man, him an' me'd do business. There's no risk if the fella can keep his mouth shut. An' if he doesn't, the Guards'll have him up for coinin' as well as me." Mickle thrust his cupped hands into the sunlight. "In light like that, I often showed a hundred coins—all like babbies new-born."

Mickle strutted a few steps.

"You've money set aside to bury you," he said loudly. "So have I. I was a farmer's son in West Cork. My father died in a strait-jacket on account of a bank. God's curse on every banker in the world! They left me a tramp on the Irish roads. Every copper my ould fella earned, they closed on it. I swore I'd get level with the banks. I'm not asking you for your money, decent man. I'm askin' you for the service of it, like the service of a stallion ass or a Yorkshire boar. With my gladar box . . ."

"Your what?"

Mickle hobbled out to the road, rummaged on the floor of the cart around the old woman's skirt, and took out a tin box daubed a smoky black.

"I have him!" he muttered up into Poll-Poll's sleepy face.

From inside his coat he took the two coins and placed them in the box. Poll-Poll again closed her eyes. Mickle looked along the bog road before hobbling into the cottage again.

"I put raw metal into this box last night," he told the countryman. "I'll open it now to see if the coins have set." As he opened the box, the pair of half-crowns fell out. "Keep 'em for luck," he said. He pushed the coins into the countryman's hand. The other looked hard at the horse on each coin, then turned them over and looked at the harp.

"I'll be off now," Mickle said.

The cottier came to his feet. "Coinin' is a mad game," he said. "But I'm with you!"

"I wouldn't doubt you."

The old fellow shuffled down to the bedroom; Mickle heard the squeak of a lifted board. The countryman returned with a faded five-pound note in his hand. "How do I know you'll come back?" he quavered.

"I'll leave you my box," Mickle scolded, "and my bar o' silver: I'll have to come back for them."

"Fair enough!"

As Mickle stretched out his hand to take the treasury note, the other drew back his hand. "I'll scribble down my name an' address," he said, "for fear you'd lose my whereabouts."

Turning his back on Mickle, he took an old envelope from the top shelf of the dresser. From a lower shelf he took a demand note for rates, tore it in two, and with a stump of a pencil began ponderously to write.

The bedroom door had swung open; through the doorway Mickle could see a table littered with tattered books. He saw a board sprung from the floor. He narrowed his eyes on the old man's back. Books! he thought. Is this fella a fool or a scholar?

The countryman had turned. He took the piece of paper on which he had written his name and address and prepared to place the paper and treasury note in the blue envelope.

"Is that your woman?" he asked.

Mickle looked out the window, in time to see Poll-Poll recovering from pitching forward. Both men laughed. The countryman handed Mickle the closed envelope. "My money and address," he said. "You'll be sure to come back?"

Mickle handed over the box and the solder. "Hide it under the floor," he said. "I'll be back in a week. Don't tell your secret to a tree. . . ."

"G'wan out, mare!" Mickle said as he clambered into the car.

"Did yeh score?" Poll-Poll asked.

"I scored!"

"How much?"

"A flim. The Midlands are full o' goms."

The old woman gurgled a tuneless song. They rode on into the setting sun. "My throat is kiln-dry," Poll-Poll said presently.

"Ditto!" said Mickle.

They came to a little public house sitting under elms Mickle swung the black mare off the roadway. "We'll bring a bottle or two for Martin an' the lassie," Poll-Poll said.

It was cool in the barroom. A pair of red-faced farmers with buttons on the crowns of their tweed caps, their arms folded, sat on a yellow stool. Pint glasses of stout were beside them. On the arrival of the tinker pair, the couple brightened; it was as if two Toby jugs had come to life.

The publican had a hooked nose and a network of veins on his cheekbones. His movements had no grace: it was clear that he was more a farmer than a barman.

"What do ye want?" he asked gruffly.

"Two pints o' porter," Mickle said.

As the publican placed the first drink before the tinker pair, the foam ran out over his fingers and down on to the counter. Mickle licked his lips. With an effort of self-control he waited until the second drink was before them. The publican set his hands, one at each side of the glasses. "*Spon-du-lix!*" he said.

Mickle threw the blue envelope on the counter. "Take it out o' that!" he said. As the publican began to fumble the envelope open, Mickle grabbed his glass; Poll-Poll hers. As the drink poured down their throats, the pair of countrymen watched admiringly. When Mickle set down his glass, it was three-quarters empty. Poll-Poll's drink was half gone as, with a snort, she lowered it from her mouth.

"What the hell's this?" the publican roared.

He had taken out the torn demand note and was searching the empty envelope. "Damn-all else here," he said.

Reading from the back of the demand note: "*This tinker is a hook.*" Then, "What do ye mean?" he roared.

Mickle backed towards the door. "I was done!" he pleaded.

The countrymen went off into bubbling laughter.

The publican took up a mallet used for tapping half-barrels. "Pay for your porter!" he bellowed. His wife came out of the kitchen. "Tom! Remember what the doctor told you!"

"To hell with the doctor! I've been gypped."

He came out the door of the snug and cut off the tinkers' retreat. The mallet swung loosely from his hand.

"Pay for the drinks!"

Poll-Poll put up her elbow defensively. Mickle backed behind her. "Give him the half-crowns," Poll-Poll ordered her mate.

"I gave the *sham* the half-crowns too," Mickle said.

"Apostolic Father!" said Poll-Poll.

"Buh-huh-huh!" said the countrymen. "You'll burst a blood vessel!" the publican's wife screamed at her husband. In the kitchen a child began to yell. Somewhere a kettle boiled over. A sheepdog appeared and, sniffing tinker, began to bark furiously. A cat, hitherto unseen, clawed upwards on a shelf and set bottles rocking. "Burb-urb-urb!" gurgled the countrymen, collapsing against each other.

"Ye, too!" screamed the publican in their direction.

"For the children's sake . . ." roared the wife.

She came between the tinkers and her husband. "Out through the kitchen!" she flung over her shoulder.

Poll-Poll and Mickle turned tail and bundled through the kitchen. The publican's wife flung her arms around her husband. "To-o-o-m!" she pleaded. The sheepdog came racing at the tinker pair's heels—somehow Mickle and Poll-Poll succeeded in scrabbling aboard the vehicle. Mickle swung the mare's head around. As if the urgency were contagious, the animal broke into the travesty of a trot as she moved downroad.

Still standing in water, his body hidden by the trunk of a tree, Martin crouched against the bank.

"A *pair* o' priests," Breda said.

"Lovin' God!"

"One is in black. The other is in brown; likely he's a monk from the monastery beyond."

"Monk or monkey, let them pass.'

"Martin!"

"What?"

"This is my chance to get the Confinement Cord. The monks here bless it. With that around my waist, I'll be safe."

"You want me to lose the fish?"

"I must have the cord!"

"In an' out o' hell with you!"

"Sssh! They're right beside us."

Father Melody led the old Franciscan monk with him along the lakeshore. Now and again the two old men came to a halt. Father Melody looked up: the Franciscan, who was a head above him, bent down, whereupon Father Melody clutched the other's head in his spread-fingered hands and shouted into the monk's ear.

His great beads rattling from his fingers, the old Franciscan closed his mouth, nodded his comprehension, and the pair resumed their slow walk.

Under his splayed feet the monk's sandals were huge. A stubble of grey beard was on his face. His cingulum was soiled and his robe faded. Wire-framed spectacles sat upon his nose. When they were close to Breda, but had as yet failed to see her, Father Melody stopped, clutched the other's bowed head, and shouted, "With all their novelties, they'll banjax the Church!"

"Be sure of it!" the Franciscan said solemnly.

"Where do they leave the grace of God?"

"Nowhere."

"They'll make the Church modern—and literal!"

"And destroy it."

"I'd rather have people believe in the magic of Puss-in-Boots than in nothing at all."

"Me, too."

"A chatting cat argues another existence—what we stand for."

"You've said it!"

"Fathers!" Breda blurted. She bobbed her knee in greeting.

Father Melody's face was the first to soften. "God bless you . . ." then, "Ma'am," he added. Breda's eyes fell to examine the monk's sandals.

"She's looking at my sandals," the old Franciscan complained.

"She is, indeed," said Father Melody.

"The creak of those sandals was heard through Irish history," Father Gabriel said in a loud voice.

"That's right, Father!" said Breda.

"Sandals like those were worn by the Four Masters, who wrote the story of this country."

"True for you, Father!"

"We had houses galore in Ireland. We had Buttevant, Timoleague, Bundrowes, Multyfarnham, and Killarney town. We had a house in Youghal in the lifetime of St. Francis himself. Isn't that something to boast about?"

"Be sure of it, Father."

The old Franciscan thrust his head forward. "Do you agree with canned food?" he asked.

" 'Tis handy, Father," Breda said.

To Father Melody, "What does she say?"

Clutching the other's head, Father Melody shouted, "She says 'tis handy."

"She's wrong! The food gets time to think inside the canisters. Another thing—I don't believe in using small words where big ones will do. Anticosmopolitanarianism, procrastination, disestablishment—those are words guaranteed to pulverize a congregation."

The monk drew a big breath. "I'm Gabriel," he told Breda in a meek tone of voice. "Who're you?"

"Don't answer!" Father Melody shouted. "I'll tell your pedigree."

The Jesuit walked round Breda. "By the shape of your skull," he said, "you're a Kerry Brien."

"That's the dam's half of me." Breda laughed.

"The other half is . . ." Father Melody went on, ". . . Steady the Greys! . . . Driscoll? No . . . Casey? No . . . McDonagh? No . . . Carty? No . . . hi-diddle-dee . . . that tumble o' hair . . . hi-diddle-dom-dom . . . a Cork and Kerry Gilligan!"

"Gilligan is right, Father."

"I was right!" the Jesuit shouted at the Franciscan.

"Married to Dick Claffey's son," Breda went on. "And I know your name, Father, though I never laid eyes on you before."

"You do?"

"You're Father Melodeon from the city of Dublin."

The Jesuit clutched the friar's head to tell him what Breda had said.

"Good girl yourself!" chortled Father Gabriel. Addressing Breda, Father Gabriel asked, "You're not taking notice of our queerness?"

"Not a bit!"

"The young priests are all in Lima, Cebu, or Tanganyika, fighting God's war. We're left at home—the Chelsea Pensioners of the Catholic Church." He drew himself up like a soldier.

"What are you doing so far out of your run?" the Jesuit asked Breda.

"We're off home, Father, for my babby to be born."

"Breast-feed your child," the Franciscan shouted.

"You hear him!" Father Melody stressed. "The Lord God never gave women tin cans as organs of nutrition. From that it's only a step to the test-tube infant."

"That's a fact, Father. What I was goin' to ask the holy father . . ."

"Where's your man?" Father Melody asked.

"Foragin'."

"For what?"

"This, that, an' th' other."

"Tell him to be careful foraging around here."

"Travellers like us got leave from the Lord to take what wasn't nailed down," Breda said with a smile.

"News for the Jesuits!" Father Gabriel laughed. "The fella who lives there," he said, nodding in the direction of a crumbling mansion, "is a martinet. Do you know what a martinet is?"

Breda looked up at the apples peeping over the ivied wall.

"My husband's name is Martin, Father," she said.

Martin dodged fully behind the tree.

"A martinet is a disciplinarian—do you understand?" Father Melody explained.

"I do, Father."

"You don't, Father," the Jesuit mimicked. "What do you want?"

"The safe-confinement cord. The monks bless it."

"Is it for snatching fish you want it?"

"As God is my judge . . ."

"This fella is half doting like myself. Call to the monastery. Ask for Father Angelus."

"I can't do that."

"Why not?"

"Once you've started a journey, it's unlucky to turn back."

"Unlucky!" Father Melody rushed at the Franciscan and thrust his hands through holes in the other's robe. He brought out a knotted white cord. "You're in luck!" he told Breda. "Probably got it for some other woman and forgot to deliver it. The cord I mean—not the baby."

Breda and Father Melody laughed together.

"On your knees, girl," the Jesuit said sternly.

Breda slipped to her knees. She eased the shawl down on her shoulders and threw back her head until the line of her throat was taut. Her fingers raised the tendrils of hair off her face. Her forehead came level with the cingulum about the monk's bulging stomach. The friar took out a tattered book and began to read. The girl's eyes grew tranced. Father Gabriel placed the cord on the girl's shoulder.

The west was turning red; the air held the first of the night's chill.

Reading, the friar's personality had changed. He seemed immense; by contrast, the Jesuit grew small. The sweat of excitement glistened on the girl's face. The circles of light from the monk's spectacles were over her.

Watching them round the tree trunk, Martin's eyes hardened.

As the monk scrawled a cross over Breda's head, Father Melody shouted a loud "Amen!" Breda kissed the knotted cord that the friar held to her lips. She then tied it around her waist. As she came to her feet, "I haven't a copper to give you, Father," she said.

"What is she saying now?" the old monk asked.

"She has no offering for you," Father Melody yelled.

"I'll give her a kick in the tail!" The Franciscan started off, then turned to say, "Take care to wipe the fish scales off the grass."

"Pass the word to the troops in the front line," Father Melody added.

Both priests winked at Breda; Breda answered their wink with an affectionate smile. She continued to look after them. She recalled that she hadn't knelt before a priest since the morning of her wedding.

(6)

        At daybreak on the wedding morning, Poll-Poll had taken Breda in a cart and jogged up into the hills.

As they travelled, there was no conversation between the old woman and the girl who was to marry her son. They came to a place where a stream barged down from the heights to scoop a pool on the roadside. Brimming from the pool, the water fanned into a shallow spread that crossed the road and clattered to a lake far below.

Here Poll-Poll drew the animal to a halt and grunted to indicate the pool.

Standing on the flat rock at the side of the pool, Breda began shyly to take off her clothes. Poll-Poll seated herself on the edge of the great stone. She took out a short-stemmed clay pipe, lighted it, and began to draw noisily on it. "Sit down!" she said, when she saw the girl standing with only her shift clinging to her body.

Breda sat down beside the old woman.

Poll-Poll sucked on her pipe.

"You an' him ag'in' everybody else," she said at last, "an' don't forget it. Be at his side in fightin' or in fun. If you don't be in your rightful place, there's another woman who'll be there in your stead. If you fall out with your husband a thousand times a day, make up with him as many times again. You hear me, girl?"

"I do."

Breda watched the old woman sharply; it was the first time she had seen beyond the crone's face.

"A man needs his woman as he needs his right hand," Poll-Poll went on. "Without us, the best of men are childer. As I mention childer, never forget that they are all ours: we want only the loan of a man to put us goin'. At times even the most balanced of men go crazy," she said. "When that happens to your man, don't screech like a chicken; lie low until the trouble's over an' then pretend that nothin' was ever wrong. Never let a man see the end of your mystery: hold the bone an' the dog'll follow you. Let crawlers say what they like, but life is fair. At times it runs like a runaway horse. But if you hold the reins of life till they burn to the bone, the whore of a runaway is sure to stop. Things will turn as lucky for you then as they were unlucky before."

The old woman hawked in her throat and spat on the cress beside her boots.

Through an opening at the foot of the dry wall on the other side of the road, Breda could see a rectangle of the valley far below and beyond it the morning smoke rising from the town.

Poll-Poll's pipe had gone out. She lighted it slowly and sucked until again it drew smoke.

"Say 'sir' to Civic Guards, and praise them. Bob your knee to priests—they carry God in their pockets. Be churched after your first baby—an unchurched woman brings tears to the threshold. Never sing: *The Pretty Girl Milking Her Cow*—it's a song that's cursed. Keep dry in your foot an' head—I seen the finest women swept off the Irish roads by consumption.

"For couples with houses," Poll-Poll went on, "trouble begins in one of three rooms—the dinin' room, the sittin' room, or the bedroom. For us on the roads, with ne'er a room, that means that a man can fault his wife in one of three ways—in preparin' food, in conversin', or in makin' love. So, if things go wrong between you an' him, ask yourself in which of the three rooms you're makin' your mistake."

Poll-Poll groaned, rose, hobbled to the cart, and returned with a bar of red soap and a coarse towel. These she threw on the rock beside the girl. As she looked into the pool her face smiled in such a manner as cracked her features into unsuspected wrinkles.

"I washed myself in that pool three times," she said, "the mornin's I was tied to each of three men."

The old woman began to chuckle. She turned away. "In with you!" she said harshly.

Breda slipped off her shift. Her arms clasped about her breasts, she shivered as she lowered herself into the pool. Sucking contentedly at her pipe, Poll-Poll looked away.

131

Her eyes closed, Breda sat motionless in the water. When her body had grown accustomed to the cold, she leaned back so that the water flowing from the rock shelf above spilled over her upturned face. Now and again she opened her eyes to look up into the green upper air. From beside the pool came a smell of heather growing from pockets of soggy peat. Behind the mountains was a suffusion of red. The water continued harmlessly to assault the girl's head and shoulders. Her wet hair clung to her skull. As she began to rub the awkward bar of soap to her neck and shoulders, bubbles formed and broke beside her body. Above her, mountain sheep bleated. Once or twice the bit in the cob's mouth jingled. Poll-Poll continued to suck at her pipe.

At last Breda came out of the pool and, standing on the flat rock, began to towel her goosefleshed body. Gradually she seemed to lose her sense of shyness. Like a terrier in wet grass, she nuzzled her head in the folds of the towel.

As if noting the change in the girl's attitude, Poll-Poll looked purposefully up and took in every detail of the girl's body. Breda's eyes, emerging from the towel, steadied to meet Poll-Poll's gaze.

Poll-Poll thrust the pipe into a pocket of her skirt, went to the cart, took out a parcel and, opening it, took out an assortment of clothes, some old and washed, others pink and new but unmistakeably of a bygone fashion.

There was a high-heeled pair of shoes in lizard skin that looked almost new. Breda had a struggle to don some of the garments; neither she nor the old woman was sure how they were worn. The girl then combed out her hair. She tightened a leather belt around her waist. From a second parcel in the cart she shook a new lightweight tartan shawl and, biting off the price tag, threw the garment around her

132

shoulders. Her skull, lacking the fluff of her hair, as yet seemed small. " 'Twill be dry by the time we get down," Poll-Poll said, with reference to the girl's hair. "Let's be off!"

Breda donned her earrings and bangles. She braced her body and took in air fully through her nostrils. She balled up her old clothes and shoes and pushed them down into a furze scrub by the roadway. She glanced down at the spire of the cathedral before joining Poll-Poll in the cart.

(7)

"My shawl!" Breda said, after they had eaten.

"What about it?" Martin asked. He looked out on the lake.

"It's colours are green and red—the colours of the leaves and the apples inside the orchard wall."

Martin squatted against a tree trunk. He lighted a cigarette butt and drew heavily on it.

"Let down your hair," he said.

Breda laughed. "What do you see in my old hair?"

"Let it down!"

"There was never such a man!" Smiling, Breda drew the pins from her hair and let it tumble about her shoulders. " 'Twill be bothersome puttin' back," she said.

Martin swung round on to his knees and ran his fingers through the hair. He separated the plaits and coils and then, pushing the freed mass of it together, caressed it with his fingers.

"What with the kid, my hair has lost light," Breda tested.

133

"No," he said. He was absorbed with what his fingers were doing.

"Why do you do it?" she asked.

"It's payment for my day."

"Payment?"

"Yes! It's like the treasure house of a king."

"You'd rather me than her?"

"Than who?"

"Than her you know?"

"Than who I know?"

"McQueen." Martin's fingers had ceased to caress the hair. "Lie to me, Martin," Breda pleaded, "if needs be, but tell that you'd rather me."

Heavily, "I'd rather you." Then, "What's on you now?"

"I'm worse off than before. I shouldn't have said about the lie."

"Bees, the tides, a woman's mind," he said, "three things no man can understand."

"You hate me for the way I am?"

"I like you better the way you are."

"You do?"

"Aye. You're like a head of corn that's about to shed. You're like a ripe marra on its side. You're like all things that break in the autumn world."

"I never thought your mind could be like that," she said. "What'll you buy me when the kid is come?"

"A brooch, maybe."

"No brooch!"

"Why so?"

"You bought a brooch for her. I seen it on her blouse."

"All right—no brooch."

He stayed on his knees beside her, his hands dead on the flat of his thighs.

134

After a pause: "If I'm denied an apple now," Breda said slyly, "the child'll cry for apples all his days."

Martin came to his feet, thrust his hands into his fob pockets, and stalked away a few paces. "You'll make no fool o' me," he growled.

"The trees are droopin' to the ground."

"You'll make no fool o' me."

For a time, Breda did not speak.

Across the lake, the sun was balanced on a low hill. The objects close to the tinker pair took on a hem of pink.

Martin suddenly cried out. He leaped for the wall, grasped an ivy branch, and pulled himself up. Peeping over the wall, he hesitated for a moment; then he went over and in. Breda scrambled to her feet. "Throw 'em out!" she shouted. "I'll catch 'em in my shawl."

Martin's head appeared above her. "They're flamin' ripe," he said, dropping a few apples, which Breda gathered. His ears caught the sound of Mickle's mare approaching. "Don't pretend I'm here," he said.

Biting into an apple, Breda sank to the ground.

Mickle and Poll-Poll drove up. The mare was dragging slowly. The old couple descended from the vehicle.

"I have a blind boil comin' where my pants sits tight," Mickle complained. "The mare is threatened with every disease in the world. We're be't!"

Poll-Poll glanced at Breda. "Hushabye, baby!" she sang provocatively as she waddled forward.

"Ach!" Mickle said.

As he limped towards the lake, an apple crunched off his poll. He swung around.

"No more o' that!" he shouted at Breda.

"You're ravin'," Breda replied, burying her laughter in a bite of apple.

Poll-Poll had turned away. A flung apple whistled past her ear. "Kid or no kid," the old woman shouted, "I'll drag your head of hair!"

Breda rocked back and forth with glee.

Martin's head appeared above the orchard wall. "Hey!" he shouted. Then the air was filled with falling apples. "Hey!" Apples, falling, crunching, rolling, hopping, and halting. Breda held out her shawl and caught some of the flying fruit. Much of it eluded her. "Hey!" Martin shouted, all the while throwing like a madman.

Mickle and Poll-Poll began reluctantly to laugh as again the sky rained apples. Still it was "Hey! Hey!" from behind the wall. "Peaches, too!" Martin shouted, his face framed in ivy, momentarily appearing. The shower of apples continued to make an almost continuous thudding around the three tinkers. At last, flung full-armed by Martin, a single apple sailed high into the evening sky and fell into the lake some distance from the shore.

Martin was down off the wall like a monkey.

"Spread the shawl!" he shouted to Breda. To Mickle and Poll-Poll, "Come on, cripples!"

All four squatted on the ground, around the shawl. "Wait!" Martin said. From his bulging pockets he drew four ripe peaches and gave them to Breda. Breda dug her teeth into the flesh of a fruit. "Um!" she breathed. "That'll loosen the child. . . ."

Martin laughed as he saw the juice run over Breda's chin. He tumbled more peaches on the ground by her knees, then spread his hands as if calling for recess.

"We'll race to see who'll ate the most," he said. "Apples for us three and peaches for Breda. Ready . . . Steady . . . Go!"

The sun was a disc slipping into a slot beyond the hills

behind the lake. The light it left as residue was compounded of green, red, violet, and bilious yellow edged to left and right with a warm pink. The four tinkers gorged themselves. For once there was no menacing form in the darkness with its growl of, "Ye'll have to move on."

After a while Mickle got up and indicated that he was moving downward to where he and Poll-Poll would make camp.

Mickle looked at the sky to the southwest. He belched as if to call attention to himself. Martin's eyes were on the ground. Breda began to gather the telltale apple cores and, rising, spilled them into a nearby scrub. The unbroken apples she gathered in her dress and hid in the cart. Again she squatted.

As Mickle hawked in his throat, the other three looked at him simultaneously. "Tomorrow the Goat goes up!" he said.

Breda looked at Martin, whose gaze was still fast on the ground. "I'll hit the hay," Poll-Poll growled.

She rolled over, clawed the grass, and coming cumbersomely to her feet, moved away. With a glance at the young couple, Mickle followed.

(8)

After Martin had rolled into the camp, Breda remained seated on the grass and gazed out onto the darkening lake. There was a weak moon.

Presently she looked along the roadway and saw an odd-coloured light moving through the dusk. The light drew nearer. She made out the figure of a boy: from his right hand hung a Chinese lantern in which a lighting candle glowed.

The boy—he was five years of age or so—walked carefully and solemnly; his eyes were fixed on the light that glowed through the paper sides of the lantern. Above him hung the green evening sky.

Slurring his shoes, his eyes preoccupied, the boy came forward until he was close to Breda.

He came to a halt beside her. Lifting his solemn eyes from the lantern, he looked at her. He then gazed solemnly at the ragbag of clothes spread on the bushes. Neither spoke. Breda looked from the lantern dangling from the boy's hand to his neat brown shoes. The boy dropped his eyes and began slowly to walk on.

Breda's eyes followed him. *"Tome soobla!"* she said to herself. "Lovely boy!" she added. She looked out onto the lake.

Martin was motionless in the tent. The dew gathered on the rim of Breda's shawl; she drew her head down into its cowl. With the passing years, Dawloon willing, there would be one, two, three, four, five, six, and more children to fill the empty cart. These would keep her company when Martin was away.

The first child was important, she told herself. When the hips had learned their business, the other children would be little trouble.

The children would romp in summer, but they could be hurt in winter. Her face tightened. Was there some way in which she could put her shawl around the unborn? So that they would not suffer as the Donaghy children had suffered in the snow. The Chinese lantern in the boy's hand had brought it back to her.

It had happened somewhere over the hills that lay across the lake. A little to the northwest, perhaps, and near the seashore, but not near enough for the sea thaw to affect the rocky land.

On their way to the North, she and Martin had pitched their camp a short distance from two caravans that were lodged face to face. The place they were in was called Burren, a barren stretch of stone walls enclosing thousands of small fields.

One morning Martin and herself awoke to find the world white and the east wind spitting pins into their faces.

It was their first experience of rough weather together. Across the bay the Galway mountains carried white caps. The sea was seen suddenly cut clearly apart from the land.

They came out of the camp and began lighting a fire. True for Cromwell: the place lacked water enough to drown a man, timber to hang him, or clay to cover his corpse.

A countryman clumped past. He had a red plastic bucket on his arm. "Ye're hardy hoors!" he called cheerily. After the meal of scraps, she and Martin had burrowed fiercely into the straw in the tent. When they awoke in the afternoon, they saw the glare of the snow through the canvas. Breda drew aside the flap to watch the polka dots fall from a pewter-coloured sky and move slantwise against the stone fences of the fields.

It continued to snow by day and freeze by night. "Maaa!" the sheep complained from the high ground. It was the only sound that broke the silence.

Day merged with night and night with day: day and night were of one piece and that had a dull metallic glare. From base to top, on its northeastern edge, a telegraph pole carried a line of rime that grew thicker by the hour.

The twigs on the bushes were finely drawn in silver. The snow froze as stiff as sugar. Once, somewhere, a motorcar churned, stopped, and fell silent.

Mickle and Poll-Poll, anticipating the bad weather, had holed up in the nearest County Home. The schoolhouses of the country were closed. The mountain children scuttled past the tent like bear cubs. Day after day the merciless wind blew. Thrushes and starlings hopped about the opening of the tent. Martin found a dead gull beside the camp—Breda tried to boil it, but the brew proved smelly and oily. As she slung it away, other gulls flew over her uttering hunger cries.

Blundering through drifts, Martin led Tomboy to a sheltered corner of a field; there he fettered the animal. Later he risked stealing an armful of hay from a smallholder's haggard. As he floundered back to where Tomboy was, he hoped that the snow would fall quickly and cover his tracks. On the road back to the camp he raided a potato pit and covered the breaches with handfuls of snow.

He had difficulty in finding the camp: tent and cart were indistinguishable from the sheeted landscape. It was the first time this had happened to him. His pockets and cap full of potatoes, Martin was about to enter the tent when he heard a child crying downroad. The following morning he told Breda of the cry. She had started up immediately.

"What is it?" he asked.

"You should have told me."

She stood in the snow-tamped space before the camp mouth and looked down the road. The wind blanched her face. For a long while she looked in the direction of the two caravans.

Carrying his bucket, the countryman crunched by. The stubble on his face was rimed, and his eyebrows were snow-laden. "Hardy hoors!" he said with a grin, and passed on.

Nothing else moved in the landscape. On her way to the caravans, Breda fell several times. The edge of her hand was bleeding. She sucked it. Beside the caravans she stood for a moment, listening. She looked up. No smoke came from the tilted tin chimneys.

In the lee of a tea chest under the nearest wagon, a half-collie bitch had littered. As a matter of duty, the animal showed her teeth; the lips stayed wide on the starved mouth. On the snowy space between the caravans, birds hopped like rats. Their feathers were fluffed out to give them a false appearance of plumpness.

Breda knocked on the door of one of the caravans. After a time the door opened a little. A smell of stale air met her. The chill face of a woman showed.

"*Gammy thálosc!*" Breda said in gammon.

"Aye! It's a bad day," the woman said. She waited.

"How're ye doin'?"

The woman shrugged.

Peering in, Breda saw children piled everywhere. She read hardship in their eyes. The woman's gaze shifted to the other wagon. Breda turned, went to it, and lifted the latch. There was a horde of children inside.

"*Their Maderum's in the keengup,*" she heard the other woman say, "*Gather misslied!*" Mother in the hospital, the father gone: the words sunk home in Breda.

The foetid air that hung about the children was almost unbearable. They pressed forward to the doorway. Their lips smiled in a way reminiscent of the collie bitch showing her teeth.

Entering the caravan, Breda choked back the first vomit of morning sickness. The fire in the stove had long since quenched. There were seven children in all; the eldest was

141

a girl of eight years or so; the youngest, buttocks upwards, was crawling wanly on the floor.

That night, Breda slept with the children, huddling them around her. The knife blades of the wind came through the laths of the end of the caravan. "What's your name?" they asked. "Breda . . . Breda Claffey," she said. "Your *jeels* is *loshte* to the *feen?*" the eldest girl wanted to know. "Aye!" Breda said. "I'm married to the man."

In the morning, Martin chopped timber with a slasher-head and somehow got the stove going. Again he stole potatoes from the pits. The children grabbed the potatoes out of the bubbling water and ate them, jackets and all. They looked up for more.

Still the iron wind blew. The countryside was deadly beautiful. The unreal serial of days and nights went by, days into weeks, weeks into a month and more. Breda and the children huddled closer together. One more day, she told herself, sucking her festered hand.

Looking down from a bridge, Martin saw a dead kelt on the ice below freewater. He recovered the fish and boiled a section of it in a blackened gallon. The cooked fish gave the children diarrhoea. They relieved themselves on the floor of the vehicle.

At night the lanterns showed on the hills, as the farmers searched for their sheep. Martin continued to forage and supply as best he could. The falling snow traced the arbitrary currents of air. Everywhere, sound had died.

When at last it seemed that the children would soon be as dead as the kelt or the gull, a man came staggering up the road. He had a sack on his back. It was the man of the plastic bucket.

"Hey, there!" he shouted. Breda opened the caravan door. "I own a shop," he said, in a voice that had hysteria in it. "I can't sleep with thinkin' of ye." The sack was full of groceries. There was a pot of marmalade. The children scooped it out in fistfuls. They quarrelled as, with grimy fingers, they pushed it into their mouths.

Then, wholly unexpectedly, the wind ceased to blow. The air grew warm. It began to rain softly.

From under the bridge came a clanking and crackling of ice breaking up. After a day or two the snow had melted everywhere, except on the northeast planes of the hills. The mother of the children returned. She was hospital fat. She did not thank Breda, nor did Breda expect thanks. The mother brought Children's Allowance money and groceries. The children greeted her hilariously.

A day later the children were in the Store, dancing abandonedly against a background of red and green buckets. Bitch and pups played on the roadway. The missing father returned. His eyes were red and insane. He had no excuses to make; he simply took his place as head of the family, and glared Breda and Martin away. The last Breda recalled of them was to see one of the boys walking past her with a candle lighting in a Chinese lantern.

Martin and Breda, with the old couple following, had moved northward along the west coast. About them was the thrust of spring. It was implied in the buds that everywhere grew too large for their sheaths. Martin looked at his wife with a keen delight. Breda was conscious of this and was happy.

On the lakeside, Breda rose from the grass. The summer darkness had fallen as she was recalling the snow. She entered the tent and lay down beside her husband.

143

The stars, the wan moon, the dead fire, the stretch of lake. The warm night air. The plop of a rising fish. The blue-white bloom, too, on the green half-cylinder of the camp.

"Put your arm around me, Martin," Breda said.

Slowly Martin did so.

"You're restless," she said. "Settle yourself for sleep."

"There's somethin' naggin' at your mind, Martin. Your body is like a struck drum. The most of our journey is over now. Is it somethin' I said or done?"

"No!"

"Are you awake, Martin?"

"Aye!"

"It's all the drivin' you done, isn't it? That's what's keepin' you from sleepin'?"

"Aye."

After a pause and a sigh: "On most nights, an' we lyin' like this, your toes talk to my toes. That's how I can tell what's on your mind, without you tellin' me. Tonight your toes aren't talkin' to my toes at all—it's as if they were strangers."

Martin did not answer.

"Martin!"

"Huh?"

"Are you listenin'?"

"I am."

"Our children will go to school like the children of the *shams*, won't they? They'll take a flask with hot cocoa in it? An' wear high rubber boots? An' keep their luncheons in glassy paper?" Fiercely, "Won't they?"

'Aye."

"An' learn to read properly?"

"Aye."

The woman tightened her body into a reassured ball.

"Martin!"

"Huh?"

"Is it breakin' for day?"

"No."

"Martin!"

"Huh?"

The girl's hand came backwards to grip the outside of her husband's thigh. "Is Puck Fair troublin' you? Answer me, Martin?"

"No."

The girl's hand clawed deeper into the man's flesh, "You're sure?"

"I'm sure!"

"Martin!"

"Eh?"

"Mornin' is in the sky. I'm afraid. Give me your hand."

Martin gave his wife his hand. After holding it tremblingly for a while, she pinned it against her body. "Feel life!" she said. Then, fiercely: "Your hand is on the child, Martin. Swear by him that you won't go to Puck."

Martin tried to pull away his hand, but the girl pressed it firmly against her. Straining her neck, she looked back at him. "Say 'I swear it!' " she said.

"I swear it!" Martin said.

FOUR

The South is gay and friendly, if the North
* is hard and cold.*
—They'd rather roam the Southland than own a
* purse of gold.*
And the gayest place in Ireland all, in North
* and South alike,*
Is the blazin' Fair that men call Puck, an' to hell
* with the Honey Spike!*

(1)

Breda sat on a porter barrel, deep in an arch-way off the square.

Through the mouth of the archway she saw the shawls glow in the late afternoon sunlight as the young women moved through the fairday crowds.

Some of the tinker girls carried borrowed infants. The infants took in the details of the hurly-burly with eyes equal to the violent sensations.

A year ago, Breda reflected, here at Puck Fair I was one of these girls. My body was then empty, and vaguely ached to be filled; my body is now full, and aches to be emptied.

As we swayed back to the camp together, Martin had his arm about me. In a place by the river, where ponies were tied, he told me that, after we were married, he would break out of his cut, and see what the rest of Ireland was like.

Above us, the stars stood up in the sky.

Breda eased the shawl back from her head and looked at the mountains to the south. Judging by the height of the sun above the hills, she reckoned that it would soon be evening.

Behind the mountains is the place I am going to, she told herself. I'm near enough to Dunkerron now and I'm not going to be baulked. And yet, somehow, I don't seem to care whether I go or stay.

I know! she told herself: Martin has broken his word. That's what women are for—to be fooled and broken. It's only an idiot girl quarrels with that law. And fooled and broken I'll be again—like all women—as long as my body is fit for childbearing.

As they drew closer to Kerry, Martin and Breda found the roads thronged with cattle. Some of the beasts had their tails and horns decorated in honour of King Puck.

The procession of flat carts flying past, harness bells ringing, brasses glinting, tinkers yelling, as well as motorcars and lorries hooting—all seemed to make Martin, with his faded cart and bedraggled pony, his stubbled face and his drab young wife, feel that he was out of place in the common mood of joy.

His face set as a horse-drawn caravan came up behind them; his eyes gave little indication that he had seen Winifred McQueen at the doorway. Breda had recognised the caravan at once; as it raced past she looked down at the road edge.

At a crossroads Martin had jerked the pony's head towards the west. Breda took the decision without reproach.

Deep in the archway the pub had extended into a barroom. Breda was seated almost at the gable end of this annex—her feet resting on a stone fallen from a wall. The backroad petered out in a scramble of sheds. At the end of the blind lane Tomboy stood listless beside the cart.

For Breda, this was a point of vantage: here she could keep in touch with the mountains and the barroom; through the archway she could see the base of the seventy-foot-high platform on top of which the goat would be enthroned, with, at the moment, dancers weaving on the lowest of its three platforms.

Loudspeakers cannonaded into sound that blotted out the *tap-tap* of sticks beating on the backs of black Kerry cattle.

In Breda's head the din went round and round.

Country lads lurched into the archway; grabbing their hands tinker girls began to gabble prophecy, but the country lads whooped and pinned the girls against the wall. Expertly, each girl slipped out of the country lad's grasp; then, ruffled as a hen is ruffled by a cock, she began the fortune-telling ritual all over again.

In the barroom the crowd had begun to howl a ballad. The poster in the window proclaiming the crowning of Ireland's only king—King Puck—shuddered as the perforated tin behind it resounded to a thump. The barroom door swung open and the crash of a breaking drinking glass was heard.

As the last line of the song was being chorussed, Breda's eyes tightened. She waited until the end of the next verse; again the woman's voice came riding in above the roar of men's voices.

The McQueen woman is inside, Breda told herself.

A few drinks, Martin had said, and then he'd resume his journey. Hadn't he deserved a drink after the long road?

Breda looked down at the ground; there were nights when she had awoken in terror from the dream of sitting where she now sat. She fancied she could still see on the cobbles the little loch of her father's blood. She realized that that which had terrified her since childhood had lost the ability to move her.

Isn't that stranger than all? she told herself. I have returned to the house of the ghost to find that the ghost has gone.

She began to urge herself to care. After a time she thought she had some success with her self-upbraiding.

How am I to leap over these mountains in time for my child to be born in the place I want him to see light? She struggled to force the problem to the forefront of her mind. Try as she would, she found herself unable to succeed.

(2)

The leading article of *The Western Cry*, a provincial Irish weekly newspaper dated August 10th read as follows:

A problem clamours for the attention of the Irish people. It is a sociological problem with overtones of a religious and national nature. The problem is the fate and conduct of the Irish itinerants, those 10,000 tinkers, tramps and down-and-outs who roam our roads without any acquaintance with Christian standards of behaviour.

Superficially these are a picturesque (and picaresque) people whose way of life finds champions among pseudoliterati who ape the slovenliness indigenous to these folk and who even flirt with their lawlessness in a clumsy attempt to achieve popular acceptance for the equation of liberty and license.

The matter was brought forcefully into focus a week or so ago in a Connaught town when a tinker horde terrorized a law-abiding community for six ghastly hours.

One elderly lady, who had been a missionary's wife in the Far East (having endured three years' internment under the Japanese), described it as follows:

In all the horrors of war, I have never witnessed such savagery.

The episode we refer to began with a violent argument between two female members of rival clans. The resultant fisticuffs between these amazons spread.

Scores of hirsute, ragged men joined in hand-to-hand fighting: iron bars, broken bottles and sticks were freely used.

Some of the female combatants were enceinte. The men fought as if possessed by all the demons in hell.

One of the Gardaí, a zealous young officer who had arrived in the village the previous day on his first appointment subsequent to the completion of his period of training, received such a blow as necessitated his having sixteen stitches inserted in his scalp in a Galway hospital.

What a truly Christian welcome for this non-drinker and non-smoker!

Were it not for the return of the Parish Priest from a sick call, we believe that nothing, except the death of many of the combatants, could have set a period to this bloody hooliganism.

When the battle had ended, scarcely a window was left unsmashed in the streets of the town. Barrels of porter were stolen, hoisted into springcarts and driven off in the direction of the Joyce Country.

The large body of Gardaí drafted into the area are experiencing difficulty in procuring assistance from the country people, who stubbornly conceal vital information.

Thoughtful citizens are apprehensive lest conduct of this nature is likely to recur at a certain traditional fair, the first of whose three days of roystering opens even as our readers scan these lines.

If so, we feel compelled to ask this question:

How long is Ireland, once the Island of Saints and

Scholars, whence missionaries have taken a gentle Message to the ends of the earth, to endorse such ferocity, such ruffianism, such atrocious conduct, that, in their sum, argue the breakdown of our society into the Stygian gloom of anarchy?

(3)

It was in a country church he had got the idea of the riddles. Riddles were the daddy-of-all.

Poetry was good company, too. That is, for an old fella by himself. So were the birds and animals of the ditches; before he rolled his body into a ball a hedgehog was a gentleman. Brown paper pressed flat against the chest was good to keep out winter cold. Benediction of a Sunday night was lovely: the priest, dressed as in the cloth of heaven, standing in the smoke of the thurible, his voice going lah-lah-lah, that was . . . superb!

Dodging the cattle and horses, Dickybird, the tramp, shuffled by the walls of the crowded town.

Under his soiled raincoat and caught securely in his armpit was a small folding table. His lips moving, a flimsy mauve scarf falling almost to the ground from his throat, Dickybird moved on. His bland face was governed by the dark pupils of his eyes. The grease and sweat of his forehead had soaked through the band of his hat.

Everywhere he went he met people jealous of his riddles.

The way to make up riddles was easy—and hard. Instead of saying the plain words, all you had to do was to chant the rhythm to lah-lah-lah . . . and let the hearers puzzle them out as best they could.

The more you were alone, the more you realised that

everyone was insane. Being alone was like sitting in an empty picture house; only, at times what was on the screen broke the frame and went careering through the dark building. Locomotives came steaming into your face. Flames were licking the roof. Waves of the sea were cresting and breaking . . .

"Hello, Dickybird! Spin us a riddle!"

"Dickybird! Act the gull!"

"Come on, ould canary! Let's hear you pipin'."

Dickybird shuffled on. He did not want to mingle with riffraff. He didn't want attention called to his table. One day he had won thirty shillings at the three-card trick. No one laid bets with him now. Danger everywhere! Puck Fair was lousy with Guards. Their flashy harness was on all sides.

Dickybird stopped to watch a parrot on a pick-and-win man's shoulder. As someone jeered at him, he moved on. "Chuck it, Dickybird!" the flyboys said. "Your fingers are all thumbs. Rattle up a riddle instead." They shouldered him roughly.

Once on this very day in this town of Puck—the year before last it was—a shoulder-thrust had brought him to his knees. Then they ran away: the shoddy gets who were afraid he'd take out his book and curse them.

What did these porter-soaked tinkers know of Paderewski in his villa by Lake Geneva where his wife bred coloured table fowl? What did they know of the fauna of Ethiopia or the mating habits of the water bok? What did they know of the cannibals of New Guinea who placed the smoked corpses of their grandmothers on racks in the hills above their village homes?

A long motorcar drew up beside the kerb. A tourist and his wife stepped out.

The man raised his eyes to the high goat platform. With a bird glance to left and right, Dickybird placed the open table on the pavement before the tourist.

The tramp began to manipulate the three cards on the green baize.

The tourist's wife came round from the rear of the vehicle and joined her husband. Ignoring Dickybird, the couple went up the hill. The old tramp lifted his head. Smelling perfume, his nose twitched. Slithering on the dung-sleazy pavement, a bunch of cattle blundered towards him. Dickybird snatched up his table and hopped away. He dodged past the platform and moved out of the sunlight into the shadow of the archway.

Beside the barroom door he opened his table and began to intone:

"It's not this card and it's not that card. No, sir: this is the one you've got to find. Find her for a shilling or a crown, sir. Remember, sir, it's the picture card you've got to find. . . ."

By the side of the green baize, the mauve scarf fell to the ground. As the barroom door opened, the singing blared out. When again it closed, the music was muted.

"Ladies and gentlemen, it's fair, square, and aboveboard. It's your eyes versus the quickness of my hands. This is the card you've got to find. Find it for nothing: find it for a crown."

Manipulating the greasy cards, the old hands moved over the baize. No one paid him attention.

"Dickybird!"

The tramp glanced over his shoulder. At first he could not see the speaker. Breda's face, partly concealed in the hood of her shawl, was turned away from him.

"Take care the Guards don't catch you!" It was a friendly voice. It was the voice of a woman.

"Guards!" Dickybird said with dignity. "The word offends me." He resumed his playing. From time to time he glanced over his shoulder at the mouth of the archway.

"How are you, Dickybird?" the woman asked.

"Who are you?"

Breda drew the shawl down from her face.

Dickybird snatched up his table by lifting the baize so that the two legs snapped shut. He walked quietly in a circle that ended close to the girl.

"I know you not!" he said.

He turned away indignantly; then, as if struck by a pang of memory, turned back. He looked more closely at Breda. His face cracked up into an odd affection and sanity.

"Breda Gilligan!" he breathed. "My godchild—Breda Claffey now." He blinked recurrently. Almost angrily: "A child no longer. A woman!" The sane look ebbed from his face. The eyes grew darker. Watching him, Breda's lips outbulged in a way that made her expression ugly. "Beauty does not boil the pot!" the tramp snapped.

Angrily he resumed his playing of the three cards.

"Chant a riddle and raise up my heart," Breda said softly.

"A riddle?"

Breda nodded.

Again, Dickybird snatched up the table. "I have a riddle!" he said in an odd chant. "So listen to the puzzle in the riddle that I'll riddle now."

"I'm ready!"

Dickybird declaimed: "Lah-lah lah, lah, lah; lah lah lah lah; lahlah lah laaah!" Eagerly, "You have it now?"

157

"That's a hard riddle, Dickybird."

"It's cut in stone above a poet's grave high in a windy corner of the north and west."

"You'll have to tell me the answer."

The old man began to intone, to the *lah* rhythm: *"Cast a cold eye, on life, on death: Horseman, pass by!"* Suddenly, "I'm a great scholar, amn't I?"

"You are, indeed."

In the square, a bunch of cobs rattled past. Tinker boys were clinging to the manes of the leaders.

"I wish my horseman would pass by," Breda said. "Did you see Martin?"

"I have another riddle," Dickybird said. " 'Twas in the reading books of the schools of long ago."

"School it out for me."

The hieratic stance. The intonation to *lah*. "You'll give it up?" As Breda nodded: *"The hollow winds begin to blow, the clouds look black, the glass is low.* I'm a prime scholar, amn't I?"

"Had Martin drink taken?" Breda asked.

"He had his share!" Snatching off his black hat, to reveal his polished head, "A holy riddle now," Dickybird said. In a burst of sunshine the blue posts of the goat's platform grew bluer still. The saffron *bratacha* of the dancers also took light. Onstage, the end of an accordion slung silver into the heart of the fair. Licking a red ice-lollipop, an old woman, her mouth open, stopped to look in at the tramp.

Dickybird began to declaim.

"That's the best riddle yet," Breda said. "I'll give that up, too."

"Woe to them that are with child and that give suck in those days," Dickybird chanted. *"For there shall be great*

tribulation such as has not been seen since the beginning of the world. I'm a great scholar, amn't I?"

"You're a scholar, no doubt," Breda said. "Is Winifred McQueen here?"

Dickybird glanced over the perforated tin in the barroom window. Turning, he rolled his eyes to indicate that he had seen Winifred McQueen inside.

Breda brought her shawl up over her head.

The tramp opened his table and looked down at it. He then glanced at the girl's face. Breda raised her eyes to the hills. "Behind that mountain is Dunkerron?" she asked.

"You're going there?"

Breda nodded. "Today?" Again Breda nodded. Dickybird tucked his table under his arm and shuffled to the mouth of the archway. Almost hopping, he returned. "You'd best be off at once!" he said.

"If Martin's drunk, he won't take me," Breda said. "And Mickle an' Poll-Poll, if their mare has come this far, will likely end tonight in jail. I'd go by myself but it might come on me on the road." She paused. "Would you drive me to the Spike?"

Dickybird made no answer.

"Would you?"

"I seen him put a hoop on your finger."

"You won't drive me, so?"

" 'To have and to hold: In sickness and in trouble'—I heard that cant too." The tramp's face was artful. "I caught an eel that had a sucker for a mouth and holes drilled in his head."

"You stood for me when I was baptised."

"*The veil that hides the future was woven by the Angel of Mercy.*"

159

"You promised God that you'd help me."

"One morning near Black Valley, on the Kerry Hills I strode.

I heard a woman moaning in a holding by the road . . ."

"You daft bastard!"

Dickybird resumed his game. There was a grace to the way he showed and concealed the faces of the playing cards.

Breda looked over the low wall to the loop of the river with the mile-long file of caravans beginning just below the bridge. The sunlight was bright on the gravel of the river strands. On a midstream island, a swan, dressing her feathers, shone with startling whiteness.

Breda wondered if it was the same swan she had seen on the morning of the wedding.

(4)

She and Martin had knelt before the high altar. Martin was dressed in a cheap blue suit, with a yellow tie. Breda, her wrists heavy with bangles, wore the lightweight shawl.

Shafting down through the stained-glass windows of the sanctuary, sunlight added a brilliance that was of a piece with the brilliance of the shawl.

The pews nearest the Communion rails were filled with tinkers. The men's hair was tousled and sunbleached. They were unsure whether to sit or kneel or squat, what to do with their hats or caps, or where to place their boots.

The eyes of the women, half hidden in their shawls, were the eyes of birds. The tinker children talked loudly, mostly of mares and dogs.

The children then began to play "Tig" and run from each other, their shouts of sham terror and glee drawing echoes from the roof of the nave. The sacristan, a lame man with a stiff-fronted collar, hobbled out along the Communion rails. "Hush, you barbarians!" he said. "Shame!"

The Archbishop came on the altar to offer the Nuptial Mass. The tinkers knelt in the silence of pride and awe.

As the couple were being married, Winifred McQueen entered by a door at the back of the cathedral. Leaning against a pillar, she watched the ceremony. On her face was a look of cold amusement.

At the moment of mutual acceptance, a Claffey child, pulling at her mother's blouse, said loudly, "Mommaw! Look!"

Winifred answered the woman's backward stare with a look of contempt. Other Claffey women then looked back. They saw that Winifred had removed the kerchief from her head. Seeing this, some of the Gilligan women half rose as if to leave their places. The Archbishop's eyes strayed momentarily from the ceremony.

Winifred swaggered out of the cathedral. In the hallway, she tied a knot in her kerchief and pulled fiercely on the kerchief ends.

People who had been to early Mass hurried home and told of the tinker wedding. They spoke of the caravans and springcarts, the ponies, goats, asses, and mongrels that filled Cathedral Close. It was memorable, they said, to see the Archbishop towering above the bride and bridegroom.

In their hundreds the townspeople gathered in front of the cathedral.

As Martin and Breda came out, there was a racket of humans and animals.

The Reverend Mother of the Convent sent a hunchbacked girl to present Breda with a bouquet of roses. In his shop at the edge of the Close, a butcher took a leg of mutton from a hook and, wrapping it in brown paper, sent his boy to fling it into the bridal cart. The Chairman of the Urban Council, a shoemaker with lines on his face, put on his Sunday coat and shook hands with the newly married pair. The Superintendent of the Guards, dressed in his court-day uniform (he had prosecuted three-fourths of the wedding party for a variety of petty crimes), afterwards wondered how he had found himself in the middle of a tattered assembly wishing the tinker couple the best of luck.

Martin and Breda were hoisted into the cart. Mickle flung his hat against the ground.

"Did I keep my word?" he shouted.

"You did!" all replied.

"Is this a weddin' that'll live for ever in the mind o' man?"

"Be sure it is!"

The townspeople roared approval of Mickle's antics. Poll-Poll began to shed tears.

The tinkers continued to rejoice. Seated in the newly painted cart, with Tomboy between the shafts, Martin and Breda looked shy.

As Martin gathered up the reins, Mickle turned to the townspeople. "Once we were kings," he roared.

He dug in his trousers pocket and after a struggle withdrew his clenched fist. Throwing a fistful of coppers into the air, "We had beggars at our gates, too!" he crowed.

The tinker children scrambled for the rolling money.

Breda continued to hold her quiet smile. "Off with ye!"

162

Poll-Poll said, giving the cob a whack. Tinkers and towns-people gave a cheer. Tomboy galloped away in the direction of the hills.

As they crossed the bridge, Breda saw a swan dressing her feathers in an island in midstream.

(5)

It was somewhere in the Midlands, as they jogged towards the South.

The grass tennis court lay length on to the road and between it and the graceful house. The sound of tennis racquet striking a ball pocked the country silence. Everywhere the trees were full-leaved.

"Forty-love!" a young woman's voice called.

Breda raised her head and muttered something. Martin drew the weary cob to a halt. A swarm of flies gathered around Tomboy's head. There was a break in the foliage through which Breda could peer.

"You're losin' time," Martin said. Breda did not answer.

A fine-limbed fair-haired girl, watched by her partner, raced to the base line and recovered a difficult ball. A tall young man returned it—his partner, a chubby girl, stood on guard at the net. The ball shuttled; after a good recovery it soared high above the court.

The tall young man put all his strength into an overhand smash. Racing sidelong to return it, the fair-haired girl sliced the ball so that it flew over the lattice-wire fence and clubbed dully down into the canvas in the cart.

Breda grabbed the ball and pushed it down inside her blouse.

"G'wan out!" Martin said at once. The cob had difficulty in starting.

163

The fair-haired girl came hurrying through a gate; searching for the ball, she glanced up and down the road. She then noticed the vehicle moving off. Placing her racquet on the wall and shouting to her companions, "I'll be back!" she mounted a lady's bicycle and set off in pursuit of the cart.

"Stop, please!" she said, as she drew level with the cob.

Martin drew the animal to a halt. The girl set her bicycle against the fence. Breda noted the girl's flushed face, her braided hair, her white linen frock and the leather belt around her waist.

"Have you seen a ball?" the girl asked, breathlessly.

Martin shook his head.

"Have *you* seen it?" Marjorie was addressing Breda.

"No, Miss!"

"Has it fallen into the cart?" the girl asked.

"It didn't fall into the cart," Breda said. There was silence for a few moments.

Raising herself on tiptoe, Marjorie looked into the vehicle. She saw only the straw and the clutter of canvas, the rods and utensils.

"It's a new ball!" the girl insisted.

No reply.

"You have my ball!" the girl blurted. "Please give it to me."

"You're wrongin' us," Martin said. "G'wan out, Tomboy!" The cob began to move.

The girl caught the bridle and forced the cob to halt. Martin got down from the side of the cart. "Easy, Miss!" he said, his eyes suddenly wild.

"If you admit having it," the girl said, "you may keep it."

"We never seen your ball," Martin said.

164

"My father is a doctor. He has always been good to you travellers."

Martin began leading the animal along the road. The girl walked at the other side of the cob's head. "However far you go," she said, "I'll follow you."

For some time they proceeded like this, Martin at one side of the cob's head, the angry girl at the other, both holding a ring of the bridle.

As Martin turned to leap onto the side of the vehicle, the girl again tugged the cob to a halt.

Martin's breath came shorter. There was a hint of madness in his eyes. The girl stood mutinously at the animal's head.

Suddenly, the girl left the cob's head and, walking towards the vehicle, looked into Breda's face. Her gaze stroked down the tinker woman's body. Their eyes locked.

"I'm sorry!" the girl said, then turned and moved away.

Dully, Martin watched her walk back to where she had left her bicycle. Breda noted the girl's dress and carriage, her braided hair, her neck, back, and seat, her bare and slender ankles. She watched her mount the bicycle and ride back to the court. She then saw that Martin, too, was watching.

Breda looked at the swarm of flies around the cob's head. "Put a branch in the bridle," she told her husband.

Martin broke off a branch of a stunted oak growing on the fence, thrust it inside the forehead band, then leaped onto the wing of the cart.

Tomboy shambled on.

Would there never be an end to this swarm of tramps and tourists, of half-baked artists with beards and woven belts, mixed up with crazy countrymen?

Patrolling the fair, Garda Sergeant Gilfallen muttered to himself.

Bandy-legged couples on tandems, city blackguards, returned emigrants, and travelling girls dressed like fish lures. The inhabitants of this country weren't even civilized. On the Green a Pakistani was telling a crowd that, before darkness fell, he'd float in air; watching him was a party of Chinese students, their attitude indicating terror of the Irishry.

Thumbs traditionally hooked in the flaps of his breast pockets, the Sergeant strolled on.

This abomination of desolation—God grant it would end in peace. For everyone else Puck Fair was an annual bit of gas; for him it meant responsibility and trouble.

The Sergeant sighed. Trouble? It was like walking through a powder magazine with a lighted candle in one's hand. For this one week the attention of Ireland, and Great Britain, too, was focussed on this town that otherwise was as sleepy as a Mexican village. Crowning a randy goat! The country boys out for a bit of razzle-dazzle, but the reporters warmed things up for their news-starved readers. "Goat Worship!" "Phallic Rites!" "Bacchanalian Orgies!": these were headlines to spice the breakfasts of credulous Londoners.

Me last fair on duty, the Sergeant told himself. Out on pension next month. Might land a job as a racecourse detective. Might even . . . "Hey, you! Drive your cattle out of the chapel gate—fair or no fair, people must be allowed to say their prayers!" A neat creel of bonhams here. A drop of good blood in that mare! Cow dung everywhere underfoot. What's that Carrons the publican says about cow dung? . . . "Wherever there's cow dung, there's gold!"

The evening sun makes everything like a furze fire.

Here's a galoot dancing in hobnailed boots. . . . Pubs open for three days and three nights—is it a wonder I get a tremor in my legs? . . . "Thanks, ma'am! No apples!" Apples? I can't forget the rainy night, with the streets streaming with liquefied dung, that a rowdy overturned a cart used as a stall. Down came the cockles, winkles, seagrass, plumduff—and the apples. The old one screaming, "My lovely apples!" I helped her pick up her wares out of the dung and then . . . She pasteurised the fruit by rubbing them to the tail of her skirt, after which she replaced them on the cart for the country lads to buy—and devour. Apples? The Irish are an immunized gang.

There goes the Fair Queen . . . Sebastian's daughter, silver coronet, white dress, green ribbons . . . off to crown the goat. If right was right, 'tis my daughter Patsy should crown him. After twenty-five years among them, Kerry clannishness still calls me an imported runner. Here's a roustabout with a dead owl and a flaming newspaper. And there's a young gypsy—her earrings like drops of blood . . .

I'll stand here to see the country lads dancing a set; their football medals are jigging on their waistcoats and their navy-blue suits are white with the whitewash from the walls.

O God! Not these McQueens with their yellow eyes and yellow ties! Troublesome, quarrelsome boyos. I wish I was bindin' sheaves in my native Tipperary instead of keepin' the peace in Bedlam. Here come two Irish-Americans with their jaws plugged with gold, janitors in apartment houses on the other side and pretending to be Earls o' Heaven on this.

I'll stand here for a while. Never know what I'd see. Might even catch a pickpocket and get complimented by the District Justice.

That's my daughter Madge dancing on the stage, her plaited hair hopping on her back. Fourteen years old last Friday; the girl looks just like her mother. Breedin' breaks out through the eyes of a cat. The dance is ended. I came late. Madge smiles down at me. Amn't I good, Dad? her smile asks.

Better move on. Saunter into this archway to see how things are getting on. . . . Here's Dickybird, the rhymin' tramp, with his mauve scarf and his dirty trenchcoat. Might knock a riddle out of him, if I crept on him unawares.

"Shades!" urgently from Breda.

The whispered warning made Dickybird freeze over his card table. The Sergeant stood at the tramp's shoulder. Afraid to move or turn, Dickybird stood stockstill.

(7)

"The best man in the fair!" Mickle shouted, above the public-house din. "I'll fight him with one hand tied behind my back."

Mickle was drinking with friends, mostly Claffeys and Sherlocks.

"Drink up, Martin! Drink up, Poll-Poll!" Mickle urged. Loosely holding a pint glass of porter, he lounged against the counter.

On the street outside, a man in shirtsleeves had a green monkey on his shoulder. The man shouted, "Hoola! Are ye Catholics or Anabaptists?" The knot of spectators laughed.

"I'm Mickle Sherlock! Tied by marriage to the Claffeys and the Gilligans, too!" Mickle went on. He did a sidestep of rage. "Where are the Driscolls and the Caseys now? Where are the Coffeys and the Cartys? Where are the cross-got McQueens?"

Poll-Poll looked at him affectionately.

Seeing his reflection in a mirror, Martin set his hat to a jaunty angle and tightened his scarf knot. "A married man preenin' himself!" Poll-Poll said.

"I'll give you bright buckles and hose to the ground;
I'll give you fine petticoats flounced all around. . ."

a ballad singer sang to his own accompaniment on the ac- cordion.

The blue cart rails passing by, the lowing of cattle, the hullaballoo of the pub—for this clamour Martin's heart had ached in the stretches of Middle Ireland.

Breda? Women were always caterwaulin'. A man was en- titled to a drink. The first kid always came slow. He'd get her there in time.

Okay! Roar up, Mickle, and challenge the McQueens! McQueens? Aye! . . . likely *she* was somewhere about. Now that I've my own woman, she can go to hell. That Mc- Queen one made me dance like a monkey. Damn little I got for chasin' her—only promises. "Tomorrow or the day after" . . . that was her tune.

When she heard I was getting buckled, she got a drop. Then she started to follow me. "Didn't I promise, Martin, love?" In the cathedral she was like a devil. . . . Just the

169

same, 'tis good to think of her that night in the laneway of Limerick city.

Take another slug at your drink, Claffey. The drunker you get, the more truth will out. Isn't that the reason you headed North? Afraid of seeing the two women together? And that's the reason Breda went with you. To have you where you wouldn't meet the McQueen woman. Did you hear how her hips jerked as she went out the cathedral door? Many a night those hips of hers kept you awake. And this god-damn mother of yours—she can see into your brain. Especially when you have women in your head.

Take another pull at your drink, Claffey, but don't look the old one in the eyes. Keep lookin' into the mirror.

Martin laughed. What kind of foolishness was this? He could stand meetin' the McQueen one now, or ten women finer than her. The snow, the guns, the lake—what he had gone through with his own woman had helped to burn Winifred's picture out of his mind.

What was it Poll-Poll had said? "Son, in a few years, when ye're man an' woman, ye'll enjoy marriage to the full. A kid'll make a woman of your wife." The trout-flecked eyes of his mother . . . accurate as regards the thoughts of man. But not so accurate where women are concerned.

'Twill be O-jackin'-well-kay! Martin told himself. The drink smells good. And yet—why don't I go off with my wife now? Am I waiting for something to happen? What's holding me here?

He spat into the sand on the floor.

On the river quay below the town, Shone McQueen lay on the grass and stared morosely at the water and the reflection of tied ponies.

A young man with a dogged face, he chewed a twig, tearing its bark off with his strong teeth and spitting the pieces on the grass beside him.

Thought was like a nut pressed together in his head.

That morning he had dressed carefully. He had ridden into town: then, when excitement was beginning to boil up he had walked out of the place. Enjoy himself? With a ball of steel in his brainbox?

What had been between herself and Claffey before Claffey had married?

Even now he could see the smile of pity on her face. Pity for him—Shone McQueen. Pity to hell! Their grandmothers were sisters but they took after different families. Winifred was a McQueen; he was like his mother's people, the Donaghs.

She blew hot and cold. Together they had asked the priest to write away so that they could get married quickly. The priest had said it'd take a month to get an answer. The month was up a week ago.

Yesterday, he asked her to see about it. "When the fair is over," she said. Then came that laugh of hers. And that look of pity.

In this man-and-woman business, tinkers were straight with one another. The gypsy drop in her blood made her crooked.

One night over Rosbeigh Strand, he had dragged her out of her wagon and flung her against the fence. "You and Claffey," he had screamed. He knew that his own voice was the voice of a lunatic. The other McQueens had saved her. Even while his fingers were on her throat, she was still laughing.

If she could still have Claffey, would she throw himself

aside? If she was a slut now, wouldn't she be a double slut after they were married?

And yet, even when he was jealousy-crazed, a touch of her hand could set him right. "Have a provin' match with that one," his father had advised. When he told Winifred she'd have to put her hand on Dickybird's book and swear, her eyes had hardened.

The ball in his head would burst his skull. He was suddenly tempted to jump off the edge of the pier.

Shone McQueen rose from the grass.

He looked up at the town. In each of the bulbs strung in loops over the bridge was a spark of last sunlight. Upstream a tinker boy rode a pony into shallow water.

From the loudspeakers a woman's voice was singing:

> *"The old people say that no two were e'er wed,*
> *But one had a sorrow that never was said. . . ."*

Shone moved away from the pier. That crippled tinker girl, hanging on her timber crutch, was watching him. Did she, too, pity him? She carried an enamel basin: she had the excuse of going down to the river edge to fill it. But she was the eyes of the encampment. By the far bank two swans floated. On the island a third swan preened her feathers. On the roadway above, pipers were trying out their instruments.

Walking away, Shone beat at the tall weeds with his ash crop. The next hour would settle it. He'd not take a drink till it was solved. He wanted no trouble with the Claffeys —the McQueens had once killed a Gilligan in this town. And it was the dead man's daughter, Breda, who was married to Martin Claffey. Once the goat was up, he'd know whether he'd wed or sleep alone. He twitched his scarf, crimped his hat, and strode up the crooked pathway.

Crossing the fence, he pushed through the gathering procession and came to the stone bridge. Walking in midroad he moved against the incline to where the goat platform stood at the top of the hill. Motorcar horns blared at him; he kept his place in midroad and forced them to move around him.

From the gravel strand below, the crippled girl watched him go.

(8)

You are an old mountain billygoat among your flock of she-goats. There is sweet grass in the lee of rocks. The plains are spread below. The air is raw but wholesome.

Foxes need watching for fear they'd steal the kids. Hares are harmless. You look out for the village lads, lest they push one of the nannies into a pool, stone her to death, skin her, bury the hide in dung, to be dug up later and stretched on the frame of a gravel sieve to make a tambourine.

Apart from hazards like that, life in the rocks is the normal run of birth, mating, and death.

Climb on a crag and sniff the wind. View the world through amber eyes.

The years pass silently. Your appetite for November wanes. A young male goat watches you carefully. A young nannygoat watches him.

On one day in August each year there is excitement in the hills. Because you have dignity in your mien and movements, for you the wind reeks with hostility.

From the lowlands come roars and cries. Sunlight is reflected from car hoods on the rugged roads.

Now comes that mad band of humans. Hundreds of them. Photographers, too, and sheep dogs. The she-goats skip off into the rocks. At first, you stand royally on a rock. You watch the approaching horde. Savages! Aborigines! Your nose twitches.

When the nannies are out of sight, you take to your heels. The crazy humans begin to yell, to stumble and run, to shout, "Head him off!"

Here come the sheep dogs. For a while you outdistance your pursuers. Then you are cornered. You try to use your horns. But your heart is no longer in the fight. Violent young humans come up. One, with greasy hair, swings from your horns. With yells of victory, others bear down on you.

You are dragged down the slope. They mean no harm. You'll be back in a few days. It's just human spirits. An annual distemper that takes bipeds.

When you meet up with the human flock on the roadway, there is a huzza. Young women in the crowd, wearing ganseys and headscarves, seem as wanton as nannygoats. All crowd round and stroke your horns. Gently they tug your beard.

You find yourself riding in a decorated vehicle, presently to be borne in triumph and crowned.

Will humans ever evolve? Will they ever reach up to dignity? To majesty? To the ultimate of looking at the world through calm, amber, capric eyes?

9

Driving off after their wedding, Breda squatted in midcart: Martin sat on the sideboard, paying her little attention as he drove. Tomboy trotted along, his hooves tapping in rhythm. At the foot of the fuchsia hedges, the fallen flowers had made a red-purple edge.

In the body of the vehicle lay their possessions: tools in a budget, cooking utensils, some new, some fire-black, together with sheets of tin. Breda's uncle had given them green canvas to serve as tent; the set of rods Martin had cut to make the frame of the tent and its ridgepole were of freshly cut hazel wood.

Now and again, Breda looked hard at Martin's poll.

She now belonged to this man, just as his pony belonged to him, or his cart, or the tin measures he hammered into shape.

I belong to no one else but him, she told herself. He belongs to no one else but me. We're spancelled together till one or the other of us dies.

Her thoughts ran on:

—What kind of children will we have? Will they be brown-haired like him or fair like me?

—Is he a good man to fend for me and the children I'll have?

—Is he as good at the tinsman's trade as people say he is?

—Will I quarrel with him and make up in the fulness of love?

—His hands—what will it be like when they'll caress me?

—Will drink make him soft or vicious? Will I be able to handle him then or will he be beyond control?

—How wide and long is the Claffey's *cut?* Is he in earnest when he says he'll travel the length of Ireland?

—Is Tomboy an honest cob? Or will he pitch me and my children into a ditch?

Breda looked away from her husband. For a time she watched the bogland passing by. The landscape was enlivened by the flash of garments worn by the country people drawing out the turf. On the roadside, men were ricking it for the winter's fires. Breda allowed her tiring eyelids to fall. She found it pleasurable to ride with her eyes closed.

After a time, she opened her eyes to the full. Her mind reframed the question she had touched on already.

—How will we be when me and him make the bed of honour for the first time?

She looked at the nodding bolls of the bog cotton and at the woodbine claws showing from a thorn tree on the roadside.

The cob jogged on. At first Breda thought that they were moving upwards to enter the pass of the Reeks and bowl down to reach the southern shore. Later it was clear that Martin intended moving along in the valley bottoms where, between the streams, lay small farms of good land.

She looked up at the pass. At the other side of it lay the South she loved.

The loosestrife wagged its purple head in the lively breeze. The furze flowers glowed. After a time she saw, in the distance, a village beside a river.

They stopped for a while to eat scraps of bread and meat. As they ate they did not look into each other's faces. Nor did they speak to each other.

10

Dickybird closed the card table and stole it up underneath his trench coat. He stood staring at the ground.

"Boo!" the Sergeant shouted in the tramp's ear.

Table and cards fell to the cobbles. The Sergeant moved slowly around the rigid tramp until he was face to face with him.

"Pick up your playthings, Dickybird," the Sergeant whispered.

The tramp raised his haggard face. Suddenly he bent down and clawed cards and table under his coat. As if intending to hasten down the twisted laneway, he moved a few quick steps away.

"Not that way!" The Sergeant laughed. "That's what we call, in Greek, a cul-de-sac."

Dickybird moved towards the wall of the barroom. Standing facing the wall, he looked down along his mauve scarf. The Sergeant stalked to where Breda sat. The girl's head was hidden in her shawl. The policeman knocked softly on the bump that was Breda's poll. "Anyone at home?" he asked.

Breda made no movement.

"I saw a woman run in there," the Sergeant said, "after warning Dickybird that I was coming."

Again he knocked softly on the shawl.

A portion of Breda's face appeared.

"That's better!" the Sergeant said. "Not drinkin', eh? What's the matter with *you?*" he asked.

"Nothin', Sergeant Gilfallen."

"You know me?"

"I do."

"Why aren't you drinkin' like the rest?"

"I don't care for it, Sergeant."

"Are you sick?"

"Not sick, Sergeant."

"What are you smilin' at?"

"I just thought of somethin'."

"What is it?"

"I'm in the sickness that's better than health."

"What do you mean? . . . Ah!" The Sergeant laughed violently. "Hear that, Dickybird? A noble answer! Girl," he asked, "is it your first?"

Breda's head nodded.

"I've nine meself." Again he laughed. "When my missus is carryin' a youngster, and if she's asked how many children she has, she says "Nine, and one goin' to Mass." The Sergeant guffawed. "Let me see your face."

As Breda drew her head out of the shawl, the laughter faded from the Sergeant's face. He ran his fingertips over his right ear. "Ten stitches in my head," he said. "And a month on the flat of my back."

No longer was the Sergeant the cartooned Irish Guard, his face simian. "One row between the Gilligans and the McQueens is enough for me," he said. "Why do you have to come back here?"

"Your eldest boy is Alfred," Breda said softly. "Is he big now?"

"He's in an ecclesiastical college," the Sergeant growled. "What's that?"

"He's to be a priest."

"The day your missus washed the blood off me, he kept lookin' at me. Alfred Gilfallen—the name came back to me

178

when I saw you. Your wife fed me with broth. There were white things at the bottom of the bowl."

"Pearl barley."

"I remember a child crawlin' on the floor . . ."

"She's dancin' out there."

"I had a bath," Breda said. "Hot water, too. I sprinkled powder on myself. Your house was often before my mind —the range and the Teddy bear that made a sound when you pressed his belly." Then: "Alfred was lovely an' bold."

"If you're expectin' a kid," the Sergeant said, "why don't you move on?"

"I'll be goin' soon."

"Why not now?"

"Martin must see the Puck up."

"Do you want him rammed into clink? And released on condition that he'll go off?"

"He might be told I said to shift him," Breda said with a glance at the tramp. "I'll hold my load till the morning."

Rounding on Dickybird, the Sergeant said: "The Three-Card Trick is an offence against the Gamin' and Lotteries Act. Chant me a riddle and I'll let you go."

"A riddle?" The tramp's face was touched with incredulous joy. "It's about life, this riddle."

Dickybird took off his hat and began to chant to lah. At the mouth of the archway stood a woman, obviously an American. Behind her shoulder was a young man wearing a chauffeur's peaked cap.

After Dickybird had finished chanting, Sergeant Gilfallen shook his head.

Dickybird intoned:

179

> *O, life is temptin', and love is teasin'*
> *And both are lovely when they're quite new*
> *But as one grows older, they both grow colder*
> *And fade away like the mornin' dew.*

With a sharp look at Breda: "I'm clever now?"

"Very clever!" the Sergeant said. He began to repeat the rhyme to himself. "You're as mad as ten hatters," he told Dickybird, "but at times you make sense. This is a curse-o'-God country. Only the mad are sane, and the sane mad."

The Sergeant walked away.

In the barroom the singing came to a crescendo.

(11)

Winifred McQueen came out of the public house.

"You're back?" she said to Breda.

"I'm back."

The gypsy walked a few steps. As she moved, a string purse, heavy with coins, bobbed off her right thigh.

"Claffey here?" she asked suddenly.

"He's here."

"Did ye travel far?"

"To the Giants' Causeway."

"Were you afraid of losin' somethin' if you stayed?"

"What could I lose?"

"A bangle or a brooch. A cob—even a man!"

"The world isn't that full of robbers."

"What do you mean?"

"Nothin'." By contrast with the warm colours of her shawl, Breda's face was pale and drawn.

For a moment or two, Winifred pretended to watch the

passers-by. Uneasily she placed her hands on her hips. Her shawl remained balanced on her shoulders and bare upper arms. She laughed shortly.

"Tell him I'll see him when the goat is up," Winifred said.

"After he's had a drink, we're off."

"Tell him I said to stay!"

"Why should he stay?"

"I want him to fix up a certain thing."

"What certain thing?"

"Not what you're afraid of!"

"There's nothin' I'm afraid of. What do you want him for?"

"My name is mentioned with my second cousin. You'll mebbe be glad of that!" With a laugh balanced in equal parts between mockery and anxiety: "Shone is odd. He's jealous of the men I knew before *he* came my road."

Breda looked up at the mountains. The setting sun had dusted pollen on their flanks, leaving the recesses a deep indigo.

Over-casually, Winifred went on: " 'Before we marry,' " Shone says to me, 'there must be a provin' match.' Yeh know, after the goat is crowned, Martin an' me are to put our hands together on that ould book of Dickybird's an' swear . . ." Again the unsure laughter.

"What are ye to swear?"

"That when Martin an' me were goin' together . . . friends is all we were—you understand?"

"I understand."

"So, for your own peace o' mind, tell Martin to hang around." The laugh died. "An' if you see him before I do, advise him to swear that 'twas recitin' the litanies of the saints we were."

"We're goin' away."

"Claffey'll stay! If I'm jilted now, I'll make trouble. I might even think of hookin' him again."

"He's mine!"

"Never trust a man until he's seven years dead—where a woman is concerned." Winifred laughed. "Off with you, if you like, but let *him* here."

"I won't do that."

"Why not?"

"Because I can't."

Winifred walked over to the girl and looked at her closely. "Oh!" she said. By contrast with the other woman, Breda could have been a child caught in mischief.

The crowds in the Square outside had multiplied. The tentative skirling of the pipes was heard.

Winifred stood irresolute.

As, in the distance, the drums of the pipers' bands began to beat, Breda came to her feet. She was conscious of a force within her, intimating that presently it would take control.

"He promised on his father's soul . . ." she began.

"Off with you!" Winifred shouted.

She pushed Breda so that the girl almost fell. As Breda recovered, Winifred caught her by the wrist and swung her in an arc. "Out of the town with you!" she screamed.

Breda came to a stop close to where Dickybird stood against the wall. "I want someone on the road with me," she said. Her voice had the querulous note of a child.

"You'll not have Claffey! Shone McQueen is my last chance, an' I'll not let him go."

Breda leaned against the wall. She closed her eyes. " 'Twill ease my mind to hear Martin swear the truth," she said, with a wan smile.

The shawl fell from Winifred McQueen's shoulders. "The truth?" she screamed.

"Aye, the truth! As payment for a knot tied in a kerchief."

Shone McQueen came into the archway. He glared at the shouting women.

(12)

In the fields around the houses meadow growth was lush; on the roadside the dock leaves were as large as spades.

It was as if Martin had been saving up this village as a treat for his wife on their wedding day.

Where the houses began, the newly wed pair pitched camp on the road margin. They were close to a humpbacked five-arched bridge. The bridge was almost indistinguishable from the backdrop of rocks on the lower slopes of the mountain. Under the arches the river slid over a table of clean gravel. Tresses of weed wagged on the riverbed; at the water's edge willows trembled in silver. Hidden in the trees sat a Norman-style church in a state of gentle decay.

While Martin busied himself with the tent, Breda took her basket and walked towards the village.

She knocked at the door of a large detached house close by.

Inside the house a small dog barked hoarsely. The door was loose at the joints. Breda noticed the millstream by the side of the house and the ruined mill in the fields. She looked up at the face of the building and the chestnut tree beside it. This was once the miller's house, she told herself. Again she knocked.

The door dragged open. A woman with slender features and grey hair looked out at her. The woman wore gold-rimmed glasses; on her blouse was a mounted claw. Behind her stood a grandfather clock. At her boots a smoke-grey Pekingese croaked asthmatically.

"A bit o' help, ma'am," Breda said.

"I'm dependent on others," the woman said. Petulantly, she added, "Wait! Wait!"

She half closed the door and went into the house. Presently she returned with some bread wrapped in brown paper. Taking the bread, Breda hid it under her shawl.

The woman glanced at the ring on Breda's finger. "Are you married?" she asked.

"Yes'm," Breda said.

"When were you married?"

"This mornin', ma'am."

"You're rather young . . ." the woman said. It was an effort that trailed off.

"A grain o' tea, an' a silver bed in heaven to you," Breda chanted mechanically.

The woman began to scold the dog in an effort to get it to come inside. Breda looked down at the dog sniffing at her shoes—a blue lap dog—couldn't kill a hare or guard a camp. Not worth a damn.

"Have you a goat?" the woman asked.

Breda shook her head.

"If you have a goat, don't let it near my apple trees."

"We've no goat."

Breda went away. The door dragged to behind her; then it suddenly re-opened. "If you have a pony, you have permission to put him into the field."

"Thanks, ma'am."

As she walked along the road, Breda turned her head

sidelong; her eye corner caught a stir among the geranium flowers in a window directly over the doorway of the house. She knew that the woman was watching her. Out of sight of the house, Breda opened the parcel. Grimacing at the stale bread it contained, she pitched it over the fence.

She was luckier at the houses in the village—the people seemed glad to see her and gave her money.

When she returned with a bottle of pasteurized milk, a loaf of sliced bread, and a packet of tea, the camp was up and the fire of faggots lighting. Martin had hacked two chops from the leg of mutton. These he had laid on a stone. Breda took the wedding gifts out of the vehicle and set about opening them. She found that a box contained imitation fruit. She tested them gently with her teeth. "You'd swear the grapes were real," she said laughingly. Then she threw them into the river.

Martin took the news that they had permission to put Tomboy in the field with a grunt of satisfaction. As he went off, Breda began to prepare the meal. He returned sooner than she had anticipated.

The sky had darkened. A few drops of rain hissed in the fire. Areas of windflaw appeared on the surface of the river. A chill crept into the darkening air as they ate the meal. Afterwards Martin took out the tools and began to work on a tin vessel.

Glancing at him, Breda knew that he was uneasy.

She smiled to herself, then began to wash the delph at the river edge. After a time, Martin got up and slung his gear and half-made measure into the cart, drawing an old canvas sheet over them. He went across the road and for a time watched Tomboy grazing in the paddock beside the tall house. He then walked as far as the bridge.

On the western side of the bridge, the river rattled be-

tween gorges on its way to the far bay. The distant face of
the ocean had the colour of pewter. Martin looked up the
roadway. The lights had come up in the village.

He examined in turn the hills, the bogs upstream, the
river, the camp, the slide of the water above the bridge,
and the rain-loaded sky. The face of the river was now
beaten with raindrops. Leaping salmon fry pocked the surface of the water with rings that overlapped the ringlets
made by the raindrops.

The house by the bridge seemed to stand on tiptoe. As
he turned towards the camp, Martin too had the impression that he was being watched from an upper window.

(13)

"Put on your shawl," Shone McQueen told
Winifred, "or I'll draw my stick across your back."

There was a lull in the fair-day din.

The gypsy woman picked up her shawl. Swinging it on
her shoulders, she again displayed her breasts and buttocks
to the full. Dickybird had turned his back on the others.

"Breda Claffey!" Shone said.

"Aye."

"You know me?"

"You're McQueen."

"I'm Shone McQueen who is friendly with this one. I
want no trouble. Tell your man to be here after the Puck
is up."

Breda did not reply.

Winifred fondled Shone's shoulder. "We're missin' the
fun," she said.

Shone pushed off Winifred's hand. "I mean no disrespect," he told Breda. "There's a doubt an' it must be banished."

"I understand."

"She's on her time," Winifred told Shone. She threw the string purse up before his face. As it fell she clutched tightly on the coins. "Come on an' drink," she said. "*Her* husband will be here when you want him."

"It means a lot to me," Shone stubbornly told Breda. "The McQueens won't be lookin' for trouble. They'll be here only to see fair play."

Dickybird had begun shuffling softly out of the archway. With a cry of anger Shone strode after him and gripped him. "I'll cut your gullet if you leave," he shouted, pushing the old tramp against the wall.

Winifred slid against Shone's side and caressed him with her body. "When we're married, you'll forget everything," she said.

She placed her hands behind his poll and began stroking his head. Shone stared sleepily into her eyes. First his body slackened; then his hands, as if of their own accord, came slowly up and hooked on to her forearms.

"Every night I'll twine my arms around your neck," she whispered.

His arms grew taut. "If what I think is true, I'll twine a rope around your neck," he said. He pushed her away from him. Returning to Breda, "I'm walkin' the fields in the mornin' hours," he said.

"Martin'll stay," Breda said.

Winifred had placed her shoulder blades flush against the wall. "One minute you're finer to me than God," Shone shouted at her; "the next minute I curse the day I met you."

He walked into the barroom.

As the door closed behind him, Winifred laughed. "When all fruit fails, welcome haws," she said.

She sat on a barrel and clasped her hands between her knees. Suddenly rounding on Dickybird, "You're the one should go!" she yelled.

"Get rid of *her!*" Dickybird whined, pointing at Breda. "McQueen'll murder me if I leave."

In the distance, the pipes began fully to play. Breda felt her body respond to the rhythm of the drumbeats: it lifted as a wave lifts, prepared to tremble, to totter, and to fall.

"Her pains have started," Winifred said in a tone of triumph. Turning to Dickybird, "Have you a chant to fit her now?"

Dickybird sidled out to where he, too, could examine Breda's face and body. "Another rambler will ride into life," he said. He began to chant: *"Walk whilst you have the light, that the darkness overtake you not . . ."*

Breda spread her arms, as if vaguely searching for a stone to throw at the pair; the pains prevented her from doing so. The passing of the spasm left a remote expression on her face. She sat on the barrel.

His gait tipsy, Martin came up. "You want to go now?" he asked Breda.

"I'll wait."

"You wanted to be off before the streets were crowded!"

"I've changed my mind."

"Tomboy might go lamer still."

"I'll stay."

"I proved a man?"

"You proved that same."

"I brought you from the Causeway?"

"Aye."

"I'll have you at Dunkerron Spike at the crack o' day—if I have to hoist you on my back."

Breda lowered her head.

Turning to Winifred, Martin's eyes took her in from head to heel. "You're a good ball of a woman yet," he scoffed. "I hear you have a halter on a man. Is he as good as them that went before?"

"That wouldn't be hard for him," Winifred said quietly. "Everythin' is fixed. Only that wife of yours . . ."

"What about her?"

"She's makin' trouble between me an' him."

"What class o' trouble?"

"Nothin'll satisfy her but a match."

"Is it a football match or a boxin' match or a coursin' match she wants?"

"A provin' match!"

"For who's this provin' match?"

"For you an' me, you fool! She put it into Shone McQueen's head. To ease her mind, we'll have to put our hands together on Dickybird's holy book an' swear . . . I don't blame her, an' the way she is . . ."

Martin caught his wife, as she sprang. "You trollop outa hell!" Breda screamed.

"Lose your get an' blame me!" Winifred said.

"You want to shame me?" Martin asked his wife.

"I asked for no provin' match. She knows it well. Tell the truth, you lyin' bitch!"

"The tramp heard all," Winifred said.

Martin released Breda, and, gripping Dickybird by the lapels of the raincoat, lifted up his face. "Was it my woman or McQueen first talked about the provin' match?" he asked.

"Watch what you say!" Winifred told Dickybird.

Dickybird raised a blue-nailed forefinger. He stabbed the finger accusingly at Breda. Breda tried to claw his face, but again Martin caught and held her. "A woman's mind is a swarm of ants," he said with hard tolerance.

The music of the pipes grew louder. From the crowds came an anticipatory murmur. Breda's face was taken with terror.

"How can I born my child with noise around me?" she yelled. "Martin, for the sake of the Virgin, drive me to Dunkerron Spike!" As again Martin's grip tightened on her wrists, Breda twisted downwards till she was on her knees. "I have a curse for you," she spat at Winifred. "That you may never feel a child kickin' like a pony in your womb."

The pipe music had ceased. The drumbeats now kept a barely audible time. To Martin, Winifred said suddenly, "Whether I marry or not, tackle your cob an' drive *her* off!"

"Because *you* say?"

"Because *I* say!"

"I'll tell ye all what I'll do," Martin shouted. "I'll drink from now until mornin'. An' if I put a hand on that book I might make bits o' your weddin' plan."

"I dar' you!" Winifred shouted.

"Don't over-dar' me!" Martin released his wife's wrists and snatched a crop out of his high boot. "A stripe might cool your heat."

Shone McQueen thrust out of the pub.

"You saw him raise his stick?" Winifred shouted.

"I saw him," Shone said.

"Lash his face!"

"I'll let it pass."

The pipers began to play a Scottish march. The walls of

the streets magnified the sound. A cheer surged uphill and broke. In the public house drinkers gulped back their drinks; in the restaurants eaters gorged themselves with the remnants of meat pies. The people pushed into the streets.

Presently the archway was filled with a roaring mob of tinkers.

(14)

It was quiet in the church. The heavy doors shut out the sounds of the fair. Before the tabernacle, the sanctuary lamp had the colour of a roadside fire. Candles were alight in the candelabrum. A smell of incense lingered among the pillars. Beside the reredos were saints cut from alabaster.

A girl of nineteen knelt in a pew beside a pillar.

Direct me, God, she prayed. Is it your will that I should marry or enter a convent? Tonight I will meet. Séamus. Tonight I must decide. Give me a sign! They have told me that in the convent it will be hard on body and mind. The tinkers and their infants are so close to the heart of nature that they disturb me. Mary, Mother of God, answer my prayer.

From the street the muted yell of a tinker child reached the girl's ears. Then, its drums tapping time, the pipers' band passed outside the church.

In a narrow area off the main thoroughfare, lace curtains parted in an old shop window. A woman's face came forward.

The face swivelled to right, to left, then disappeared. Two trembling hands were seen holding a sheet of paper

191

with stamp-edging adhering to its upper edge. The hands pressed the stamp-edging against the glass of the mullioned window. The face disappeared. The hands disappeared.

A neat old man came up the street. He stopped, took spectacles from a metal case, and began to read the notice in the window. From behind the lace curtains, the woman watched him. The notice read:

ONE POUND NOTE REWARD

to anyone returning to this address, a Siamese tomcat. The cat is cream-coloured with dark-brown face and similar-coloured ears, paws and tail. A small reward will also be paid for news of the cat's death, provided the informant did not have any part in killing the animal. The cat answers to the name Niki.

Muttering to himself, the neat old man walked on. He stood outside a newsagent's and looked at the placard at the doorway. Again donning his spectacles, he read:

BORDER RAID. ONE DEAD, FIVE WOUNDED.

"Tck-tck!" said Master Horan of Farranagark.

A group of young tinkers appeared. One of them spied the eyes behind the lace curtain: he took off his soft hat and flapped it on the glass. The notice fell. The woman's eyes dilated. The tinkers laughed. Then they raced to greet the pipers.

A blind man stood against the wall. Around his neck hung a framed begging notice. He had a mug in one hand: with the other he held the end of a dog chain.

The long-tailed fox terrier had retreated behind its master's boots. It shivered

I've a safe place when the crush comes, the blind man told himself. Black glasses, a crucifix, and a greasy waistcoat—they're better to me than a farm.

"Ah, the blind!" he whined aloud. Suddenly his hold on the chain tightened. He smelled faggot smoke and sweat from old clothing. He moved backwards against a doorway.

The tinker lads crushed by. The beggar breathed freely. Now came the din of hobnailed boots; this time the smell was of milk and cow dung. With a flick of his hand, a country boy dragged open the flap of the blind man's trousers. The cursing of the beggar fumbling for his buttons mingled with the sound of the pipes.

John Patrick Kenefick, labourer, stood with one boot on each of two planks at the top of the goat platform. Beside him and across the planks was a block-and-tackle. He looked down at the packed streets.

Under his boots the planks thrummed with the movements of the dancers below. It is the first time I have been given this honour, John Patrick told himself.

Where he stood, there was no support. Disdainfully, he hitched up his breeches and tightened his belt. He was jacketless; his shirtfront was open and the air had dried the sweat on his body. Later, in the pub, some of his cronies would say, with admiration, "I seen you stand up and tighten your belt."

Looking over the rooftops, he could see his wife standing at the door of their cottage. She was shading her eyes to look up at him.

Want all your wits about you up here, he told himself.

As the goat is being hoisted if he pisses down on the celebrities there will be a guffaw. If he tumbles, there will be a national upheaval.

The spectators massing in the street grew still more taut. Every window was packed.

He could now see the bobbing sporrans of the pipers. The lorry with the howdah containing the goat was coming into view. He could clearly see the queen and her attendants. After these came the ragtag and bobtail of tinkerdom. The pipers were shrugging their green bags higher into their armpits. The drums were beating time.

For John Patrick Kenefick, labourer, this was the finest minute of the year.

A young man of nineteen, his face brick-red, walked down a roadway from the hills. Entering the rejoicing town, he marched with a soldier's step.

A change from the curséd Congo, he told himself; from a blue United Nations beret perched on the side of your head, and the faces of the women black, black, black. And, eternal Moses, the heat! The officers with their warnings on this and that and th' other. The cross-talk about changing leadership. And always the possibility of a knifeblade between the shoulder blades. And the sweat on the metal of the small arms, on the blue notepaper as one wrote home.

Here a cool Irish night of adventure to come. And the faces of the women white, white, white . . .

Near the platform, where the crowd was thickset as a hedge, he pushed forward to a place of vantage. He glanced in an archway: tinkers were like rival nations—always on the brink of war. He enjoyed the cool breeze playing across his face. The soft accents of the people was a change from Swahili.

A voice called. "Welcome home, Séamus:"—I almost said "Jambo!" Séamus told himself. Sweat, sweat, sweat, remembered from the Battle of the Tunnel. The day like an oven, the nights like an icehouse. Those tinkers are buzzing again. The pipers band is coming closer. It's like a ceremonial parade in Elizabethville . . . the same tune, too.

The young man's eyes began to scan the crowd. Where was she?

"People of Kerry and of all Ireland to the north and east . . ."

The voice from the loudspeaker blasted across the crowds.

"Into this village in the Kerry hills, from every nook and cranny in the land, we are assembled on this, the Gathering-Day of our age-old fair, to honour Ireland's one and only King—King Puck!"

Cheers like an explosion. Cheers shot with wanton hilarity.

On the first-storey platform, the as-yet-uncrowned he-goat looked out at the crowd.

"I will not waste your time—or my own—in gabbin' about nothin'. All that we have to do is what our forefathers have done since immemorial time. And that is, with suitable ceremony, to crown our King."

The girl dressed in spurious Celtic costume stepped forward. She held a polished copper crown. The he-goat gazed mutely at the girl, at the cameramen jockeying for places, at the eye of the television camera, at the stewards ordering the affairs of the coronation.

In a hush the girl's voice was heard: "Goat! With this I crown you King of Puck Fair!"

The baying of the great crowd was edged with frenzy.

On the platform voices called out: "Hold it!" "Don't take your hands away!" "A little to the left!" "Blast that guy!" "Once again!" "Smile, Mary."

Lights flashed, and an orange cape shone luminously.

The man at the microphone concluded his address:

"And now, people of Ireland, and of foreign lands, too, we'll hoist our sovereign to his throne, where for three days—and nights [violent cheers]—*he'll reign over music and song, over jollity, merriment, and devil-may-care."*

The bells on the horns of the he-goat jingled. Men vied for the honour of drawing on the ropes. The howdah began to ascend. Someone threw a head of cabbage before the goat's nose. This raised a cheer-laugh. The goat crouched to balance himself in the swaying gestatorium.

(15)

"Let me go!" Breda screamed.

"Make a passage for the girl," Winifred urged.

"She'll be all right here," Mickle insisted.

" 'Twill make a flamin' night," Poll-Poll yelled.

"For the love of Christ, Martin Claffey, take me away," Breda begged.

The tumult sent senses sprawling. Then, as the ceremony of crowning ended, there was the sudden silence of anticlimax. Shone McQueen rounded on Dickybird. "The book!" he shouted.

The mob of tinkers began to sidle. The gaiety ebbed from their eyes. Their tendency to take up groupings was almost imperceptible.

In mid-area Dickybird opened and set down his small table. With deliberation he took off his trenchcoat. As he removed his hat, one of the tinkers came forward to hold it.

The tinkers had moved outwards until there was an open space in which the tramp stood alone. Dickybird's baldness was accentuated by the black hair at the sides of his head and at his poll. The pupils of his eyes were large and dark.

From the tail of his pocket, Dickybird drew a tattered missal. He looked around at the circle of watchers. The blotted gilt of the book's edging and its soiled markers impressed the silent tinkers.

One after another, the men, except Martin, took off their headgear. The women, except Winifred, covered their hair with their shawls.

Dickybird turned over the pages.

At last he stopped and placed the open book on the table before him. He set his dirty forefinger at a point on the page.

Full-throatedly he began to chant, "Lah-lah-lah-lah . . ."

When he ceased, he looked around with an air of triumph. No one spoke. Martin's nostrils seemed to have grown huge. Winifred's head was thrown back and, for the first time, her face showed something of strain.

Solemnly Dickybird sang the solution of the riddle:

"Neither fornicators nor adulterers shall inherit the Kingdom of God."

Shone came forward. "Stand there," he told Winifred. Winifred did so. To Martin, Shone said, "Stand there." Martin pushed his crop into his high boot and idled forward a few steps.

197

Breda came to tiptoe and watched openmouthedly. Her face was faintly saffron.

"Put your right hands on the book," Dickybird ordered.

Winifred glanced at Martin's face. Casually, she placed her hand, palm downwards, on one page of the breviary. "You!" Dickybird said to Martin.

Martin flicked his hatbrim upwards, then moved a single step forward. He now showed no trace of tipsiness. As he bowed his head, his eyes roved to look at Winifred and the McQueens.

"Your hand on the book!" Shone McQueen said loudly.

Martin raised his right hand before his face. "I might," he said. "And then, again, I mightn't." He spat into his palm.

As if addressing the palm of his hand, Martin added: "Come to think of it, 'twas here the McQueens killed the father of my wife."

His hand came slowly downwards. Suddenly it snatched the ash crop out of his high boot. His toecap sent table and book flying. "McQueens to hell!" he shouted.

"Crucify 'em!" Poll-Poll yelled.

"Let the blood flow!" Mickle screeched.

Catching the stick as it bore down on his head, Shone flew at Martin's throat. The two men grappled, fell, and rolled over on the ground. The bloodied faces of the pair were seen erratically as they rolled to and fro on the cobbles. Partisans urged the fighters to kill each other.

At first there was a tendency for each man in the crowd to hold back his neighbour. In tugging Breda away from the grapple, one of the McQueens caused the melee to become general: no sooner had he laid a restraining hand on the girl than Mickle hit him on the head such a blow of a crop as sounded as if a bullock's head had been struck by a brutal herdsman.

The music of the pipes passing the archway added a note of bedlam to the scene. One of the McQueens brought Dickybird's card table down on the head of an opponent; a Gilligan tried to gouge out an opponent's eye.

The women screamed like maenads and, catching each other by the hair, tore one another to the ground. Dickybird grovelled on his knees and tried to gather the scattered leaves of his book. He had somehow managed to place his hat awry on his head.

Sergeant Gilfallen, his whistle blowing, hurried into the archway. A press of laughing, shouting country people followed.

Poll-Poll was tugging at the masonry of the low wall in an effort to prize loose a jagged stone to put in her woollen stocking, which, when swung, would provide her with a weapon of murder.

The Sergeant received a blow of a stick on the head and was sent sprawling. Seated on the ground, he continued furiously to blow his whistle. Brandishing a mallet, a bartender came out and seemed unsure whom to club. Mickle was crouched against the wall, nursing a kick in the groin. When the fighting was at its fiercest, Breda crumpled under a blow on the head. She staggered and fell on top of Dickybird.

Young Guards, their batons drawn, came shouldering through the bystanders. The fighting became three-cornered—Gilligans, McQueens, and the Guards, with a few countrymen taking a hand to keep the brew on the boil.

Dickybird, the leaves of his missal gathered, made to crawl off. Hearing behind him a sound like the mewing of a cat, he turned. He saw Breda on her knees, her eyes rolling. She was retching emptily.

The tramp dragged her to her feet. He placed his shoulder under her armpit so as to support her almost dead weight. As they lurched away, Breda, her eyes closed, was moaning. Pulling and dragging at the girl, Dickybird forced his way through the people. Somehow, Breda held her feet.

From the top of the platform, Kenefick saw the swaying pair emerge from the throng and come out on a side street. They passed Master Horan; the old schoolmaster paused to utter a *tck-tck* of disapproval at the sight of the staggering tinker girl and the tramp. At a street corner the young soldier, who had used their wake as a means of moving through the crowd, came face to face with the girl who had emerged from the church. "Séamus!" she breathed, her eyes shining.

The tramp and the girl swayed downhill; a tinker child looked up into Breda's face and smiled recognition; just then the new tennis ball dropped from beneath Breda's clothing and went rolling down the roadway. With a yelp of glee the young tinker child chased and clutched it. Without even a backward glance, she ran away back to the wagons.

Breda had tried to raise her head to follow the course of the ball, but the upended world had teetered before her. Her eyelids dropped and her head lolled. Pulled by Dickybird, she staggered on.

FIVE

'Tis a long ould day that has no dark, and a long
    ould night no dawn,
And the brothers Drink and Music,
    they end in a drunken yawn
—But Birth and Death are brothers, too:
    at times they're lick alike.
So, with Birth and Death for comrades, she
    reached the Honey Spike.

(1)

"Are you mad, Dickybird?"

"I'm stone mad, goddaughter."

"Were you always mad, Dickybird?"

"Not always."

"What made you mad?"

"A woman and three fools."

"I don't understand."

"The woman I married gave birth to three fools in a row. Their eyes bulged and they were fools. Before the fourth was born, I ran away."

"And you never went back?"

"No."

"What happened after that?"

"The voices of women drove me mad. The noise they make is in my blood always. Eyes and thighs, they're before me day and night. They never stop screechin' at me. It's their way of gettin' satisfaction."

Sitting on the floor of the cart, with Dickybird driving his hairy pony through the dark, Breda drew her hand back over her aching head. It was a moonless night with an edge to the air. They were driving south into a country of low hills.

"With me you aren't mad at all," Breda said.

"When there's only two there, I never mind. But with more than two my brain looks for leaks in my head."

The hooves of the animal sounded softly in the night.

For a time, as they drove along the road that led to the mountains, the town, with its music and lights about the goat tower, continued to sound and sparkle below them.

Then noise and lights fell away, and the world of revelry was as if it had never been.

The barrier of the Reeks rose before them and merged with the lighter darkness of the sky. At intervals along the road, cottages appeared.

"You see colours in your daftness, Dickybird?"

"Aye."

"How do you see the colours?"

"I see all things as blue and red and yellow. The blue of a cart fills the bogland. It's the same with the red of the bullfinch and the yellow of the yellowhammer."

"What else?"

"Sometimes the colours spin and turn into steam. The steam whirls in my head. I stand in the steam like a priest standin' over a pit. I walk away from myself and see myself standin' there an' bein' mad. 'Don't be mad!' I tell myself. But my tongue is wagged by someone else. I begin to talk like the priest standin' in the steam."

"How do you see the night?"

"The night is made of velvet. It has the purple colour statues wear in Lent. At times I try to stroke it, as if it was the bare shoulder of a woman."

Dickybird looked up. "If there was a young moon, I'd see it as a gold hook," he said.

"I'd see it as a hook myself," Breda said petulantly.

The wheels ground on the grit of the road.

Breda tensed, then gripped the side of the cart. Dickybird drew the animal to a slow halt and waited till the pains had eased. Afterwards he asked: "The blow on your head—is it painin' you?"

"It will pass."

"Tck! Tck!" Dickybird said to the animal.

"Give him the whip," Breda said.

After a time Dickybird said, "I sold you when the Mc-Queen one asked who wanted the provin' match."

"It doesn't matter."

"Peter sold the Carpenter."

"What Peter? What Carpenter?"

"I'll suffer for sellin' you."

"You're buyin' me back now."

"You dropped a ball; it rolled down the hill in town."

"On the road from the North there was a girl playin' with a bat. Her ball hopped into the flat."

"What did you want a ball for?"

"For the kid."

"What age would he be, before he'd play with a ball?"

"About three."

"That won't be long passin'."

"I'll get another ball." After a time: "I wouldn't like him to renege the roads an' go into a house," she said. "An' yet, I can't bear to think of him bein' out in the winter. In the end of the year he could go into a *keena* till, say, St. Patrick's Day. Then, when things'd be growin', he could go ramblin' again."

"That'd be all right."

"Will they put us off the roads? An' take our children from us?"

"Likely they will. We're the last free."

They drove on. On either side of the road boulders were piled. From below the road came the brawl of water.

"There was this monster in days of old," Dickybird said. "It had claws of bronze. It had snakes for hair. Whoever saw it turned to stone. . . ."

"God save us!" Breda said.

For a time they travelled in silence.

"Where was I born, Dickybird?"

"North of Lahinch, in Clare County. It was around the time of the Fair of the Cross."

"Poll-Poll was right. What age does that leave me?"

"Seventeen and a bit."

"Where was I christened?"

"At a naked church between Doolin and Lisdoonvarna. A woman was prayin' beside the font. Her lower eyelids were dragged down. They were blood-red."

"Had the priest a beard?"

"He had a beard. Outside of a monk, I never saw a priest with a beard before or since."

"What kind of a day was it?"

"A day of wind an' haymakin'. The houses there have roofs that are slabs of stone."

"Tell me more."

"I was walkin' from the sea. The flat car came after me. Your father hopped out. 'Can you say the Creed, Tramper?' he shouted. He was as drunk as a lord. 'I can!' I said, like a fool. 'Hop bloody well in, then, an' stand for a kid,' he says to me. I couldn't refuse. All Gilligans are crazy from the womb. Only for I standin' for you, I wouldn't be here now. While we were inside, your uncles played Solo by the side of the chapel. The priest said, 'Hurry! The sea trout are runnin'.'"

"What class of a baby was I?"

"I never noticed. I walked off. 'Come back an' wet the child,' your father said. I drank port wine in a pub near a dried-up river."

"What else?"

"That night I went to the top of Moher Cliffs, 'Wind of Eternity,' I roared, 'tell your Boss I was askin' for him.' I got a fit of laughin'."

The cart ground on.

"I tamed a robin," Dickybird began again in a low voice. "My soul went into the robin. When the robin died, my soul died."

"Why didn't you tame another robin?"

"I never bothered."

"Why didn't you whistle your soul back?"

"The robin used to lie close to my rib. I had my jacket up like this. He'd be in there, pickin' crumbs."

"Was it because of his red breast you liked the robin?"

"I couldn't say."

They came over a ridge. Above them in the Reeks the smashed surface of the world writhed and leaned up and across acres of darkness. At the crossroads, Breda said: " 'Twill be a piece out of our way, but I'd like to travel by the village. After that, you can turn left up into the high ground again."

They went on and on.

There was little traffic on the roads. After midnight a cyclist, without a light on his bicycle, went hurtling past. "Up the Puck!" he shouted as he dashed by. At last they came to the river. For some distance the road ran beside it. At the bridge near the village, Breda looked at the tall house. There was no light in its high windows.

"What brought you the long road?" Dickybird asked. "Nothin'."

"What brought you this way, I say!"

" 'Twas here Martin an' me made our first camp."

"Why didn't you say that at first?"

"When you started to talk about the robin, I thought you were off your head again."

"You thought wrong."

Breda looked over the cart side. She tried to see the big

stones amid the roadside grass. Failing to see them, she thought that perhaps the grass had grown over them.

(2)

She had placed the stones herself, trundling them forward from the edge of the blackthorn thicket and standing them carefully at the fireside.

It was their first camp. Men were ruled by habit, Breda told herself: as the stones were now, so such stones always would be while they were together.

Martin would likely query a later change.

She spread straw in the camp and drew a grey blanket over it. Bunching extra straw at the head of the shake-down, she made crude pillows.

The rain had ceased. She sat on one of the stones.

It was dusk when Martin returned. Hands deep in his pockets, he stood above her. Abruptly he sat on the idle stone and stretched out his legs. He began to look at his toecaps. Neither of them spoke.

Darkness crept over the landscape. The rain returned, more deliberate than before. Country people passed by: a girl with a hayfork on her shoulder, a man with a bale of hay rope, big-eyed children having little fish in jam jars— all in a hurry to be home. The rain hissed softly down. Presently it drummed on road and canvas. It hammered on the surface of the water.

"Go on in!" Martin said.

He came to his feet and drew old canvas over the harness in the cart. Breda crept into the tent. She lay down, faced the canvas wall, and drew up her knees.

The air in the camp was close and clean. From under

lowered eyelashes, she watched the opening. She listened to the raindrops spluttering in the fire. She smelled fresh blanket, straw, burning faggot, bruised grass, and new canvas.

Lightning lit the world. She trembled. Thunder came with the sound of iron-shod wheels rumbling over a metal bridge under which she had once encamped as a child. She fancied she could smell burnt sulphur in the air.

Martin's body darkened the opening. Then came a flash. For a moment he was black against a white sky. Behind him the thunder reverberated. The straw noised quietly under his weight as he lay down beside her.

For a time he lay on his back with his hands clasped behind his head. A cart pushed by; Breda's ear was close to the road so that the sound of the wheels was magnified. "Go on out, blast you!" the driver urged. The rain settled down in full purpose.

After a time, "It's heavy rain," Breda ventured.

"Aye," Martin said.

His eyes were angry. She'll think me a fool, he thought, for camping so close to the river. He'll think me a fool, she thought: I should have brought back much more from the village.

Darkness came fully down.

Breda thrust her hand into the straw. "The water is in!" she said. She sat up. Martin placed his hand under the blanket. The water from the road camber was sluicing under the camp.

He crawled out into the downpour and rolled the two stones into the camp, Breda sat on one, he on the other. They looked out at the rain.

Moving through the blackthorn thicket beside them, river water crackled like terriers moving through dry

209

bracken. The roar of the river mingled with the roar of the rain. Presently the pair were ankle deep in water.

I have a good man, Breda told herself; there's nothin' to fret about. I have a woman of pluck, Martin thought. Then: How far will this damn river rise?

After a time they saw a mackintoshed figure splash up to the camp; an old lantern of pricked tin stopped at the entrance and its light fell upon them. "Hurry, or the river will catch you," a voice said.

Breda recognised the woman of the tall house by the bridgehead. "We're all right, Miss," she said.

"You're not all right," the woman insisted. "Come with me."

Martin left the camp. Breda followed. Martin picked up a rope and tied one of the cartwheels to a bush. The muddy water from a blocked ditch had flooded the roadway. They splashed forward across the bridge behind the woman. They came to the door of the tall house. "Take off your shoes," the woman ordered.

Shoes in hand, they padded after her into the kitchen. The Pekingese made curious noises in its throat. The grandfather clock ticked loudly. In the kitchen a range grinned with heat. Overhead, an oil lamp gave out an amiable light. "Dry your feet on the mat," the woman said again.

Standing side by side, they did so. The woman placed her hand on Breda's shawl. "You're drenched," she said.

"It's nothin', ma'am," Breda said.

Martin hung back. The woman clucked him forward into the kitchen. "I live alone," she said. She placed the dark wet shoes on their sides in front of the fire. The sopping stockings she hung from the bars over the range. She brewed a pot of tea.

Sipping the tea, Martin took off his hat and set it on his knee. He seemed poised to run off at any moment.

"Try some biscuits," the woman said.

Martin broke the biscuits awkwardly. As pieces fell to the floor, the pet dog touched the crumbs with a long, mysterious tongue. Breda's eyes were darting here and there.

As the tinkers rose to go, the woman said, "You'll sleep here."

"We'll be all right, Miss," Breda said with a sharp look at Martin.

"Your camp is under a foot of water," the woman said. "It was a foolish place to pitch it."

Martin showed resentment. The woman lighted a candle in a blue-enamelled candlestick. She walked to the foot of the stairs. "Come along," she said.

"We'd rather be off, Miss," Breda said, halfheartedly.

"Follow me!"

The rain beat down on the leaves outside. "What next?" the great clock seemed to reiterate.

After a glance at Martin, Breda followed the woman upstairs. Martin delayed in the hallway but, as the ticking of the clock continued to reproach him, he padded upwards. On the landings the smell of geraniums was pungent.

The woman led them into a high-ceilinged room in the corner of which a brass-bobbled bed glittered. On the bed was a honeycomb bedspread: white valances with lace insertions fell to the floor. Breda's eyes rested on a washstand in a corner with its basin and graceful ewer.

The woman set down the candlestick in front of an oval mirror. "You'll be comfortable here," she said. With a loud "Good night!" she closed the door.

Martin looked up at the ceiling. Breda walked towards the mirror and admired her reflection. Her fingers touched her wet hair; she looked over her shoulder at Martin. He turned away.

Turning from the mirror, she eyed his back from heel to head. She seemed amused.

Martin drew the curtains of the window apart and placed his face close to the glass. From a loose eave chute outside, a torrent poured. He made out the white shape of Tomboy sheltering against a hedge; straining forward he could discern the swollen river racing under the arches of the bridge.

When again he turned, Breda was squatting on the bed-clothes. She stretched out her bare feet and looked at them. "My feet are white," she said. Martin did not answer.

She curled up on the honeycomb quilt and drew her shawl over her body. "Quench the candle," she said.

Testing the bed, Martin pressed and released it a few times.

"A bed is grand," Breda sighed.

Martin placed his ash crop on the occasional table at the bedside. He took off his hat and placed it across the stick. He took up the matchbox on the dressing table, opened it, and took out half the matches. These he thrust into his pocket. His eyes first roving to take in the room, he blew out the candle.

A spark lingered on the candlewick; for a time the smell of burning wick was strong in the bedroom.

Martin lay down beside his wife. His body did not touch hers. On the candlewick, the spark died. Martin lay tense and still until he knew by her breathing that Breda was asleep.

He remained motionless, his eyes trying to pierce the darkness.

(3)

Sergeant Gilfallen, his head bandaged, threw open the door of the cell and directed the rays of his torch downwards on the sprawl of ragged men.

"Out with ye!" he shouted.

The tinkers, Mickle and Martin among them, were sleeping in a tangle on the floor. At the sound of the Sergeant's voice they stirred in stupor. Some tried to rise but fell back, groaning.

A young Guard handed a bucket of water to the Sergeant. The Sergeant sloshed the water on the recumbent figures. As the water hit them, the tinkers protested with drowsy anger. A second pail of water followed. Then a third.

The tinkers staggered to their feet.

"Ye curs o' Christendom," the Sergeant said, "listen to me! I'm due to retire from the force before long. If I prosecute ye now, I'll be brought out of retiral for the Court. Only for that, I'd swear ye into jail. So, ye scruffy, dog-rough gang o' hangmen, out with ye at once!"

Friend and enemy alike, the tinkers stood glowering.

"Pull up your curséd camps," the Sergeant went on, "tackle your animals and hit the road."

Mickle came shuffling forward. He seemed suddenly to have grown very old. "We're off, Sergeant," he said, contritely.

The old fellow's voice was husky. A rivulet of blood had flowed down his upper eyelid and dried black on his cheek. He kept his fingertips pressed on the point where his thigh met his belly. He looked back at Martin, who now, standing apart from the others, was looking up through the bars at a star that showed faintly in the sky.

Shrugging their skin against the inside of their clothes, the tinkers passed out into the dark street.

For a moment Martin stood at the top of the steps outside the barracks door and surveyed the town below him. The fair had grown quiet, and the singing from the pubs was reduced to a faint boom like the noise of the sea.

Shawled tinker women appeared in all parts of the Square. Some crawled out from under the booths and came forward. Martin came to where McQueen women mingled with Gilligan and Sherlock women.

"Where's that wife o' mine?" he asked.

No one answered.

"Ye hear me?" Martin shouted.

A young girl said boldly, "I seen her go off with Dickybird."

"Was she in labour?"

"She was in labour," the girl said. "Her old head was waggin', too."

Martin stared angrily into her face, and the girl's hand went up to clutch the tennis ball hidden in her breast. As Martin's eyes left her, she said eagerly, " 'Twas me in the snow. Remember?"

Martin paid her no attention.

(4)

"What's the loveliest thing you've seen, Dickybird?" Breda asked.

The tramp looked up at the ragged sky.

"In Youghal in Cork County one September," he began, "a lot of old farmers' wives had come to the sea. They were

214

dressed in black and they had white brooches on their blouses. They sat around the walls in the room of a hotel . . ."

"Yes?"

"A pedlar from India came in and sat in the middle of the room. He opened his suitcase and took out scarves and dresses. The sun sent a light into the place. It lit the Indian's face and his scarves too."

"That was good," Breda said.

Head down, the pony was now striving upwards towards the pass.

"When my ma was lyin' in the Spike," Breda said, "she said to my father 'I'd give anythin' for a boiled rabbit.' He went away an' tried to snare a rabbit, but it was no use. He sold a gelatine X-ray box she got in the Spike. He got a bob for it an' bought a rabbit. He boiled the flesh an' carried it to her in a paper. ' 'Twas the soup I meant,' she said. He was hurt, for he had drank the soup. Her hands sweated fierce. I found the smell of death when I came into the ward."

The pony had a loose shoe, which clattered on the limestone road.

"Hup, pony!" Dickybird said.

There was no moon. The wind stirred about and died. The roadway was barely distinguishable from the surrounding countryside. As Breda stiffened and threw back her head, Dickybird drew the pony to a halt. The girl gripped on the tramp's outstretched hand.

The spasms passed. Responding to a jerk on the reins, the pony moved on.

"Talk on, godfather."

"What'll I talk about?"

"Anythin'."

The tramp said: "The days turn in the wheel of the year. One day is special to most people: it's their birthday. There's another day in the year, an' it's hidden. It will come out of the calendar an' be printed in blood. It's their death day."

"Talk on!"

"There are four hundred kinds of kisses. The noblest kiss of all is the kiss of a father for his daughter on her weddin' day. Love and its denial meet in it. The kiss of a man for his wife has terror in it. Each is frightened and wants to hide inside the body of the other."

"To have a good partner is the main thing," Breda said.

The mountain wall above them was sensed rather than seen. The mountain pass was implied by the rush of wind that slammed down on them with unexpected strength.

Breda rested her back against the tramp's knees. Dickybird's face was close to her hair. The pony seemed to crouch. The loose shoe clattered.

"It's hard to gauge the age of a nun," Dickybird said. "Age is written on the skin of the throat and at the butt of the teeth. A nun's throat is hidden under her gamp. You can't see her teeth because she never opens her mouth in idle laughin'."

"I'll see nuns at the Spike."

After a period of silence, Dickybird began again:

"The Mormons were founded by Joseph Smith, Esquire—God rest his soul. He looked for gold hidden in a hill. He was assassinated in Navaroo in Illinois. His successor was Mr. Brigham Young who led his people into the State of Utah. They were persecuted because they believed that a man had the right to many wives. . . ."

"Say somethin' else," Breda said.

Above them wisps of clouds were weaving. About them

216

boulders glared. Flanks of rock shone on the cliffsides. Water streaming over the rock flanks took the arbitrary light of the sky.

Clatter-clatter went the shoe, as the pony pressed upwards.

"A story with fun in it," Breda said suddenly.

"Will I riddle it?"

"No!"

"So Paddy the Irishman and George the Englishman and Sandy the Scotchman travelled on until they came to a public house. George was ridin' a blood horse an' Paddy was ridin' his old ass. Sandy was walkin'—he was too mean to buy an animal. At the bar, the Englishman called for a drink, paid for it and, before he drank, he said, 'Pardon me!' He ducked out the backway an' cut the tail off Paddy's ass. Paddy spotted him through a window. He didn't preten' a word. After a while Paddy slipped out an' cut open the ribs of the Englishman's horse. They all come out then. 'What happened to my horse?' George asked. 'Your horse burst his sides laughin' at my ass without a tail,' says Paddy."

"I'm glad the Irishman got the better of them," Breda said.

They journeyed on.

"Is there a life after this one, as the priests say?" Breda asked.

"Things here tell of a fuller beauty in a world to come."

"You believe it, so?"

"We know where we are; we don't know where we're goin'."

"What matters most in life?"

"Under God?"

217

"Yes."

"Cock an' hen, bull an' cow, stallion an' mare, man an' woman."

"Explain that."

"To a man, everythin' that a woman does is fit to be watched. To him, the smell of her sweat is whiskey. It was the cause of my fatherin' fools."

"This robin—did he take the place of a woman with you?"

"Could be. The bird's breast was like a blouse."

"Talk more, Dickybird; it'll pass the time."

"What'll I talk about?"

"About man an' woman."

"Life moves on the crosspiece of drake an' duck, of ram an' ewe. That crosspiece is there, although it might be beautiful an' lawful. It lies between the oldest man an' the youngest girl. Between father an' daughter. Between old bishop an' novice nun. It has no law an' every law."

The tramp tried to peer upwards at the road ahead. "When you were made, God put a note into your fist," he said then.

"How did my note read?"

" 'Pass life along!' "

"Is that all?"

"Isn't it enough? Mate, give birth, die. That's your message, woman."

After a pause, Breda asked: "If Martin or me was to lose the life an' if the other married a second time, how would we be paired off, man an' woman, on Judgement Day?"

"Mate, give birth, die . . . that's all I know."

The light over the mountain ahead indicated sky above rock.

218

The tramp laughed, then he began: "There was a king whose wife had run off with another man. 'God's curse on women,' he said—this king. He reared his daughter where no man could see her face. When she was grown a woman he took her to a fair. He showed her machinery and marvels. . . . 'What are those?' she asked, lookin' after the men. 'Geese!' the father said. At the day's end, the father asked, 'Daughter, out of the marvels of the fair, what'll I buy you?' 'Buy me a goose, Dadda!' the girl said."

"You're a gay man, Dickybird!"

A spasm came and went.

There was a lull in the din of the night. Then, from behind two crags, the winds rushed out and tried to overturn the vehicle. The frightened pony ran a few clattering steps against the incline; to Dickybird and Breda it seemed as if the fells about them had begun to rear upwards in monstrous black-and-white. Breda cried out and tried to grip the side of the cart; she pitched sideways on the floor of the vehicle and lay sprawled on her back. As a labour spasm came, she screamed for the tramp's hand; he did not wince as her nails bit into the ball of his thumb. His other hand on the reins, he tried to control the restive animal.

At last Breda released her grip and, after a struggle, succeeded in sitting up in the cart. Dickybird got out and made to lead the animal by the head.

At first it seemed as if the pony did not recognise its master, for it backed until the rear of the vehicle struck against a rock. There was a noise of splintering timber. The tramp shouted loudly.

As Dickybird led the animal towards the crest of the hill, the winds stomped to a crescendo of uproar. Water shafted down a chasm to the left. Where the pass was, two sheeredoff rocks, one on each side, parted; then pony, vehicle, tramp, and girl passed through in a stillness much as if they moved in the vortex of a whirlwind.

As the pony felt the weight of the vehicle press against its tail, it began to move briskly. Dickybird dragged on the reins and scrambled onto the sideboard of the cart. Breda, her head emerging from her shawl, smelled deeply of the soft night wind.

They went briskly downhill, the loose shoe chiming, until at last the roadside rocks came at an end.

Presently they saw the first of day edging the peaks. The landscape became suffused with light: the red raddle that branded the mountain sheep showed bright as arterial blood. Below them, in the as yet dark land, were lakes surfaced with silver. The breeze grew kindly and the holly bushes glossy. The sun crested higher above the mountains.

When Breda saw far below her the white hotel, her face broke into a smile. Her eyes searched for a meadow that tilted down to a hidden stream.

" 'Twas there!" she blurted at last.

" 'Twas there what?" Dickybird said with a start.

" 'Twas there nothin'!" the girl said sharply. The secret smile returned to her face.

(5)

Hour after hour Martin lay wide awake on the bed beside his wife.

He did not speak to Breda, nor did he touch her; he seemed satisfied to listen to her relaxed breathing as she slept.

When the rain had eased off, he cautiously drew himself up on his elbow. The shawl had slipped from the upper part of Breda's body; Martin carefully moved it over the point of her shoulder.

He then lay back again and, locking his fingers behind his head, looked up at the ceiling.

Daylight appeared in the slits of the curtains and sparkled on the brass of the bed. Martin swung noiselessly out onto the floor; groping for his hat, he knocked over the crop. Breda started at the resultant clatter, but did not seem to be fully awake. Martin held his position until he was sure that she was again asleep. He then picked up the crop, set it against the wall, and soundlessly parted the curtains.

It was as if there was a conflagration behind the mountains.

Tomboy seemed a ghostly pony; the illusion was strengthened when he disappeared into the mist wrack that hung about one corner of the paddock.

Martin craned closer to the glass. With the force of the flood the cart had swung round, but the rope binding it had held. The camp was a little awry but was still standing.

Martin turned. Breda stood at his shoulder, her face close to his face. They looked out at the mountain rim now fully daubed with flame. The peak of Carntual stood up in royal fire.

"We'll go now," Breda said.

They tiptoed downstairs. "I'll tell! I'll tell!" the grandfather clock seemed to say. In the kitchen, the Pekingese came out of a corner and made throttled noises of affection. Martin and Breda drew on their shoes and stockings.

The front door with its crotchety locks and bolts gave

them a few moments' unease; at last they succeeded in opening it. Quietly they drew the door to behind them.

On the gravel by the doorway drifted straws and twigs marked the high-water level of the flood. Slushing in silt, Breda broke camp; with quick movements of his fingers Martin tackled Tomboy to the vehicle. Husband and wife piled the gear into the cart. The ball of the sun was full as they clambered aboard.

Eager to be off, Tomboy tossed his head. As Martin drew on one rein, the cartwheel spun on a single point of rim. Then the cob broke into a gallop.

From the window of an upper room, the woman of the house watched them go. Dressed only in her nightdress, a coat hung from her shoulders; her eyes showed neither anguish nor the hope of ecstasy.

Some distance beyond the white hotel, the road dipped and curved among low trees. This was a place of intense silence, where fuchsia blossoms had begun to fall.

Martin drew the cob to a halt, leaped from the sideboard and, leading the animal on the grassy road edge, tied it by the reins to a bush. Breda came out of the vehicle and stood watching him. Entering a narrow laneway, almost choked with fuchsia bushes, Martin pushed resolutely ahead. Breda followed.

The laneway ended in a dry field of furze clumps and half-seen rocks. Martin, with Breda close behind him, crossed the field diagonally and entered a small sloping meadow in which were windrows of hay. The morning sunlight evoked a smell of dry hay and young aftergrass.

Martin went down the meadow slope to the edge of the hidden stream at its foot. Here a windrow stood close to

222

the uncut grass of the headland. He then retraced his steps up the slope and surveyed the countryside. He looked long at the walls of the hotel, which he could see through the trees.

Back in the hollow again, there was no sound except the chuckling of a secret stream. At knee-height, brambles showed small firm fruit. The stems of the sycamore leaves were wine-red. There was a smell of meadowsweet.

Martin began tugging hay from the foot of the wind-row.

Breda spread her shawl on the hay-bed. Martin stretched himself out on the hay; he lay with the hoop of his back turned towards the girl. As he grunted, Breda stretched herself behind him on the shawl.

For a time they lay without movement. Then, feigning a shiver, Breda stretched back her hand and, taking the lap of the shawl, slung it over her body, at the same time attempting to drape it over Martin's side. The lap was too short; on the pretext of giving him more of the shawl, Breda drew closer to her husband. Again she cast the lap of the shawl.

He swung to face her.

For fully five minutes Martin examined every part of the woman's features. There was something of truculence to his staring. Breda met his gaze wisely.

With her fingertips she then touched the hair at the edge of his temples. One fingertip described a small circle. For a while he seemed unmoved by the caress.

The tempo of the movement of her fingertip increased. Then, with a choked sound in his throat, he threw his arm about her and drew her body against his.

A blue moth fluttered over them.

(6)

Shouting: "Can ye go no faster?"

Shouting: "Move on there in front!"

Shouting: "Hurry, or the girl'll be lost!"

Standing behind their husbands at the doors of the sway-ing wagons, the tinker women urged the cavalcade through the night.

The clopping of unshod hooves extended over a long stretch of the mountain road; behind the vehicles straggled piebald foals and dogs of mingled breeds, their hair bristled on their backs. Tied to the wagon axles were milch goats, their swinging udders an encumbrance to their movements.

As the procession rattled onwards, the dogs barked with a furious hoarseness. The goats and kids cried out in plaintive protest.

Martin came first, with Tomboy, his lameness perforce forgotten, between the shafts. Mickle and Poll-Poll lay sprawled asleep in the body of the vehicle. After the cara-vans proper, the procession tailed off into a moving mid-den of old vehicles. The rear was brought up by a boy der-vish on a mule, who, with wild cries, tried to keep a herd of donkeys from lagging too far behind.

In the bunks at the back of the caravans, under the jig-ging lamplight, children slept soundly, their heads swing-ing like the heads of broken dolls.

A newly made gallon clattered down from the rack at the back of a wagon. It became entangled in the hooves of the horse immediately following and almost brought the animal to its knees before a fortunate hoof kick sent the vessel skittling off the roadway. The driver braked his body so resolutely that he knocked his wife sidelong on to the top of the hot stove. The woman's cries mingled with the anthem of obscenity her husband sent after the utensil.

From behind came the cries:

"Blast ye! What are ye laggin' for?"

"Drive on!"

From the windows of roadside cottages, the wives and mothers of smallholders who were still at Puck Fair peered out at the procession. "Gilligans and Claffeys on the move," they said, recognising the animals and vehicles. "Trouble somewhere when that gang's scootin'."

In his bed in a neat cottage, an old man propped himself up on his elbow to look out: " 'Tis like a weasel's funeral!" he told his grumbling wife.

The wheels ground on, hooves rattling like dice, harness bells ringing, dogs barking, goats bleating, and men roaring. Whenever there was a lag to the speed of the cavalcade, the women said, "Force the horses! D'you want to find her strainin' in a ditch?"

Martin's cart reached the pass ahead of the others.

The sun had been up for an hour or so as he leaped from the vehicle and, standing between the two rocks of the pass proper, looked along the ribbon of road that stretched to the south. There was no trace of Dickybird's cart.

Martin was bareheaded. The blood had darkened on the bristles of his face; a trickle of dried blood zigzagged down from his left earhole. The skin of his cheeks and forehead was contused.

His eyes searched the road and the landscape on either side of it. His gaze then dropped to the roadway at his feet as if he were searching for dropped grass; this he also failed to find.

In the vehicle his mother and stepfather were snoring loudly.

Martin went to the rock-piled fence on the road edge and looked down over the scree at the white hotel in its oasis of green fields. He retraced his steps on the road edge on the northern side of the pass and found on the grass a greasy square of newspaper which he concluded that Dickybird had dropped. At the foot of a protruding rock above a fresh wheel track he found a splinter of newly broken-off timber—the small smear of green paint on the rock face at cart height, matching the old green on one facet of the timber, was proof that Dickybird and Breda had passed this way.

Martin looked back at the intermittent line of shuddering canvas that stretched below and behind him; far away behind the boy herding the donkeys he saw an open cart in which sat a woman with a yellow square on her head.

He vaulted onto the sideboard and urged Tomboy forward.

Why had the woman run off like this? he asked himself. Women were foolish in the unthinking things they did. Didn't she know that all men liked play-actin'? And that, as such, it never went deep?

The thought occurred to him that his body, iron-taut as it was, was not whole: he felt as if he were one part of a worm that a spade had cut in two. And that his furious wriggling was meant to achieve a joining with the part of him that was missing.

He looked back. The first of the wagons had appeared

between the two great rocks. He tugged savagely on the reins and crashed the crop down heavily on Tomboy's back.

(7)

At the point where the rough mountain road met the coast road of tarmac, there was a lushness of growth.

Here, almost wild, were azaleas, arum lilies, palms, arbutus trees, and bamboos. Rhododendron thickets were everywhere: hydrangea clumps showed huge blooms of pink, pale blue and white.

Looking through the pine trees below the black road, Breda could see the calm green of the sea. Where the pine wall was broken, she saw tree-tufted islands reflected in the water; farther out to sea everything was hidden in a heat mist.

Her bluish lips broke into a smile. Above her, Dickybird was seemingly asleep; the cartwheels revolved easily on the tarred road.

They came to a byroad, leading upwards and away from the sea. Dickybird came to a sudden life.

Responding to a yell and a jerk of the reins, the pony took the turn with a spurt of speed that carried the cart and its occupants almost to the top of the ridge. Here the trees over the road were tall and remote, and the world they enclosed was a subaqueous green. On all sides moss drooped from walls, stones, and trees.

Below the road a river fell noisily from the rocks into a pool. Higher still the road climbed until it widened; there, flanked at one side by a lodge of spotted limestone, was the recessed gateway of the hospital.

Dickybird drew the pony to a halt beside a tree growing in the embrasure of the gateway. He got down from the vehicle.

Breda had difficulty in climbing over the side of the cart. She hitched the shawl onto her shoulders and stood looking at the iron gate. "I'm here, anyways," she said.

She looked up at the bell chain hanging beside the gate lodge. "Ring the bell," she told Dickybird. She drew her knuckle across her nostrils.

Dickybird was peering through the bars of the gate; inside, a notice was daubed on a piece of black board nailed to a spar.

"The bell!" Breda said.

Dickybird pulled on the chain; somewhere a bell rang with a dull sound.

"That should get Mollumby out of bed," Breda said.

The tramp walked away from the gate and moved to the back of the cart. Breda, her forehead bright with sweat, said urgently, "Ring it again!" Dickybird returned and again drew on the chain. Again came the dull sound of the bell ringing.

The pony moved to one side and began to tear at the bright grass.

"Mollumby is a sound sleeper," Breda said. Closing her eyes she rested her head against the trunk of the tree.

The tramp's yellow eyelids seemed to bear down over his dark pupils.

"Where are you?" Breda asked sharply.

"Here!"

"Give the chain a good tug."

Before he could do so, the door of the gate lodge opened; Mollumby, the porter, an old man wearing a grey imperial beard, his trousers pulled up over his nightshirt, came out. He was barefooted. "That's enough!" he said, in a sharp but genteel voice.

Dickybird moved away so quickly that the mauve scarf floated in the leaf-green light.

"What d'you want?" the porter asked Dickybird.

"It's her!"

"What do *you* want?" Mollumbly asked Breda.

"I want a bed."

"A bed?"

"Aye. I'm near a child."

"No bed!"

"Mr. Mollumby, sir," Breda said, as if speaking from sleep.

"What's that?"

"Get me a bed before I drop me child."

"Not here," the porter said.

"Time come, child come. Tell Mother Xavier I'm here."

"Xavier is dead. Eight months and more."

"Tell Sister Innocenta that Breda Claffey wants her at the gate."

"Innocenta? She's in Africa. Off with you!"

"Mr. Mollumby, sir. Tell whoever's in charge . . ."

"I'm in charge. I'm the Reverend Mother, the sisters, the surgeon, the physicians, the midwife, and the nurses. The whole shootin' gallery is Michael Mollumby—me!"

"I got a blow in Puck . . ."

"Read what's on the board."

"I see two of everything."

The contractions took her. She dug her nails into the bark of the tree.

Later: "I'll read the notice for you," Mollumby said, his voice wary, but not unkind.

229

He went to the gate. "This Hospital is closed. C-L-O-S-E-D, closed! Now you understand. It's locked and barred for twelve months and more."

"It's as if a nail is drivin' through my skull," Breda moaned. She leaned against the tree.

"I'm goin' back to bed," Mollumby said. To Dickybird, "If you ring that bell again, I'll brain you."

The skin of Breda's face had begun to twitch. She opened her eyes and began to laugh hysterically.

"The funniest thing I ever heard," she laughed. She lowered herself to a squatting position on the ground and, with clenched fists, began to beat the clay on either side of her. "Closed, closed, closed, closed," she repeated.

"Get her out of here," Mollumby told the tramp. To Breda, "Stop that laughin'."

"I can't!" Her voice continued going off into snatches of odd laughter. Dickybird turned to the wall and, with a dirty fingernail, began to pick mortar out of a crevice.

Breda stopped laughing. "I was laughin', sir, because I was in dread."

"In dread of what?"

"I lost the holy cord. And then . . . all the way from the Causeway, I could hear the brothers behind me."

"What brothers?"

"The brothers Birth an' Death . . . For one bare hour, sir, let me have your bed."

"No!"

"Let me lie on your bed, an' my child'll walk down the stairs of life."

"Not here!"

"My people'll make it up to you."

"Off with you!"

"Dickybird'll find me a woman. I'll wrap the child in my shawl an' walk away. I give you my word in God . . ."

Breda struggled to her feet and lurched towards the door of the lodge. "Down the stairs of life!" she screamed. Mollumby gripped her. They grappled formally, like Eastern wrestlers prior to seeking a throw. They swayed to left and right. Gradually the struggle took on a harshness that brought the grappling to a little climax; this in turn ended as Breda ceased to struggle. "If I travel on, I'll lose the life," she said. "I'll curse you with my last breath."

Still holding Breda's wrists, Mollumby fell back a step. "Mr. Mollumby," the woman said, "travellers say you're a God-fearin' man."

The porter blinked. His eyes met those of Dickybird; the tramp's fingernail was idle on the wall. As, tentatively, the porter released the girl's wrists, her shawl slipped to the ground. Mollumby looked down at her swollen body, then bent to speak into her almost asleep face.

"I've something to say. . . ."

"Hh?"

"If things go wrong, you won't blame me?"

Breda shook her head. Above the treetops a gull cried. Breda's body grew rigid. She twisted in a series of contractions. She moaned. Her hands sought the tree but failed to find it. The porter came close to her; she gripped his nightshirt below the shoulders, dug her nails into the balled-up cloth, and, writhing against his body, dragged the nightshirt open so that the grey curls on his breast showed. "The stairs of life!" she cried.

After the flow of the tide, the ebb.

"The shed where I used to keep a goat," Mollumby whispered. He indicated a lean-to at the side of his lodge.

"Is it part of the Spike?"

"Made by the same hands."

Breda's face came dreamily alive. "If your mother's soul is in Purgatory, that my prayer may set her free. Boil the kettle, sir. Dickybird will find a woman." Breda took up her shawl and, moving lightly, entered the doorway of the lean-to.

Porter and tramp turned away. Seemingly of its own volition, the door of the lean-to closed slowly.

(8)

At this point of time, in the extreme north of the country, a boy ran across the rope bridge that linked the rock of Carraig-na-Rede to the mainland. Halfway across he stopped; as the frail link swayed, he shouted to the fishermen below:

"Da! Is it true that the sea is alive with fish?"

"Come down and see!"

The father looked at the heap of still twitching salmon and said to his brother, "They must have spawned by the million in the upper fords."

Resuming his racing across the plank, the boy thought of the cowardly tinker man.

In the extreme south, a McSweeney man from Ardoughter finished his breakfast, walked to the doorway of his house, and looked out at the islands.

From behind him his wife said fretfully, "Put that damn boatrace out of your head!"

The man smiled. He hadn't been thinking of the race itself: he was thinking of the rat-like girl who had fallen into the sea.

In the dayroom of a Constabulary barracks near the border, Kenneth Yeoman sat reading a letter typed on official notepaper:

"You are hereby informed," he read, "that because of exemplary devotion to duty and bravery in the face of attack, you are promoted to the rank of Sergeant, with effect from August 1st. inst."

The young constable looked at the window. He saw between him and the glass, merging and parting, two forms: the form of the man he had killed and the form of the woman he loved. These forms receded and were replaced by the form of a pregnant tinker girl emerging from a roadside camp.

Meg Postlethwaite swung her legs over the side of the bunk and bleared out the porthole. Grey morning hung over the Liverpool docks. She sighed and said: "True for Bernard Shaw. Good health should have been contagious, and not disease."

She thought of Mickle. "Must ha' been a bright spark in his day," she told herself with a smile.

Standing at the foot of the altar in the lakeside church, Father Melody recited the opening psalm of the morning Mass. *"I will go to the Altar of my God . . ."* he intoned.

Old Father Gabriel, acting as acolyte, murmured: *"To God Who giveth joy to my youth."*

What joy? What youth? Father Melody suddenly asked himself. For me, it is disquiet and the heckling of a part of me that wishes to be free. As those others on the roads are free . . .

The old priest at his feet continued drowsily to murmur the responses.

Frank Horan awoke. Outside the window of the farmhouse bedroom a cock was crowing. He was lying on a mattress filled with feathers.

My glasses are still missing, he told himself. His thighs were swathed in bandages. The walls of the room were distempered a dark blue.

He thought of Puck Fair. This should be Binding Day. This time twelve months he had been with Peter the Fiddler in Upper Bridge Street in Killorglin. The pair of them had been up all night.

I made Peter play me "The Mason's Apron," Frank recalled. The old fiddler's fingers were trembling.

Had the Claffeys got away? Had they reached the fair in time? About now they'd be starting a second day of gaiety. "I must pay back the Claffeys," he said, "for the good turn they have done me."

An old man came into the room. He had a newspaper in his hand.

Thick-thock. Thick-thock. Backhand, overhead, recovery, smash . . . faster and faster the ball came pelting.

For the sleeping girl the game of tennis suddenly changed into a furious horserace. She was astride a black stallion galloping along a narrow mountain road. Behind her a piebald cob was gaining ground. *Thockety-thockety:* as her rival drew level, she glanced sideways and recognised the tinker girl whom she suspected of having stolen her tennis ball. The tinker girl's body was slender and her

face eagerly alive. Her hair was loose on the wind. *Thockety-thockety:* some vague winning post loomed nearer.
. . .

The sleeping girl awoke with a cry.

In the bedroom directly beneath, a young man who had been sitting up smoking in bed heard the sound. For a long time he looked up at the ceiling.

The morning sun shafted into the mahogany planes of the Archbishop's study. His Grace sat at a desk, writing.

From time to time he raised his eyes and looked at the gilt lettering on the spines of the books confronting him.

Family Planning. Birth Control . . . What attitude should the Church take up on these matters?

The whorled pillars of St. Peter's seemed to tower over him as again he wrote: again he heard the waspish whinings of the autocycles everywhere dangerous on the streets of Rome.

Every syllable, every word, every sentence must be weighed and re-weighed.

Nothing that I am to say must give scandal to those who praise the traditional pieties of my people. I need the help of the Holy Ghost.

His Grace looked down on to the garden. He thought of the young tinker couple, their hands joined as they gabbled prayers. Rather sadly, the Archbishop smiled.

In a farmhouse kitchen in the Midlands, a farm wife started cooking the breakfast. The bedroom door was ajar, and now and again she looked in at her husband, still in bed. How quickly afterwards he returns to sleep, she told herself. She began to hum a lively air. This time it will be better, she thought. The tinker girl will bring me luck.

A bull bellowed in a far field.

The morning sunlight glittered on the polished crown of the puck goat.

The animal looked from the canvas rigs below him to the scimitar of the river and the mountains. He mouthed up a cabbage leaf. As he chewed, his lips seemed to repeat: "Mad Ireland!"

The goat's eyes rested on the road edge where, the evening before, there had been a long line of wagons and caravans. "Gone!" he seemed to comment and, again, "Mad Ireland!" As he sought another leaf his nose twitched and his mouth stopped short of the cabbage head. As if attacking a presumptuous young puck, he began tentatively to butt the air.

In the bedroom of the house by the bridgehead, the woman knelt to say her morning prayers.

"I forgive everyone, O Lord," she said aloud, "even the Lannerys who injured my family in the lawsuit, and the Income Tax officers who sent my father to an untimely grave. God be good to my Aunt Julia in the city of Holyoke, Massachusetts. And also to my brother Thomas who died in infancy. God be good also to the tinker girl who slept under this roof this time twelvemonths . . . Amen!"

The Pekingese waddled in from the landing and smelled at the brown footsoles of his mistress.

The girl sat at the head of the table, drew a pad of notepaper to her, dipped a pen in an old inkbottle, and began to write:

"My dear Séamus: I've thought a lot on what we said last night and at last I have made up my mind.

"Even before I tell my father and mother, I'm going to tell you. Séamus dear: I'm going into a convent on the 1st October. I hope you get a lovely wife. . . ."

Wife? The girl stopped writing. She recalled the swollen tinker girl leaning on the tramp, and suddenly realized that the girl had not been drunk but was almost on her time.

"Wife, wife, wife . . ." the word was evocative. She began to chew the end of her pen; the pen end splintered. Wife, wife, wife, wife, wife, the girl repeated as if under hypnosis. Wife, wife, wife. The word was all-powerful.

She tore out the sheet of notepaper and tore it across.

(9)

"Priest?" Martin shouted at Mollumby. "What does she want a priest for?"

The porter raised his forearms protectively as Martin lunged towards him.

Martin stopped. His uptilted side face took on the green of his surroundings. As he turned and raced back to his own cart, the first of the other vehicles came trundling up.

"Hey!" Martin screamed at Poll-Poll, who still slept in the body of the cart.

He dug his hands into her shoulders and clawed her up to a seated position; then, gripping her wherever he could find purchase, he dragged her heavily over the side of the vehicle.

Poll-Poll found her feet with difficulty; with Martin pushing her in front of him, she waddled towards the door of the shed.

"With your filthy hands," Mollumby said, as he stood before her. "How dare you!" His voice carried a frayed authority.

A band of tinkers stood irresolute behind Poll-Poll and Martin.

"Road lice!" Mollumby said. "What do you know about hygiene or sterilization? The eyes of this girl are unequal. Her head is a whole egg with the yolk smashed inside. Get a priest at once."

As Martin gripped the porter by the throat, the man's chin and beard jutted upwards. The eyes protruded still more. Martin, growling like a dog, held his face close to the face of the porter.

Winifred McQueen came up. "Easy!" she told Martin. Indicating Poll-Poll, "Keep her out an' I'll see to your wife. My hands are clean."

"Clean!" Poll-Poll guffawed.

The tinkers growled with bitter glee. As Winifred turned on them, they fell silent.

"Take your pick who'll tend your wife," Winifred told Martin.

" 'Twould suit you if she was lost," Poll-Poll said.

Winifred's eyes blazed momentarily. "Very well," she said quietly, and turned away.

Poll-Poll entered the shed. Other tinkers came up and fell silent. Dickybird snatched off his hat and began to chant; one of Breda's uncles, standing behind him, gave the tramp a kick in the buttocks that sent him stumbling. Dickybird shuffled to the other side of the road and continued to watch the scene with bright eyes.

Martin stood in front of the gate. He was looking through the bars at the grass-grown avenue.

For a while there was silence.

Even the children and the dogs made no sound. The minor chimes of harness seemed muffled by the moss of the walls and trees. The colours of the shawls seemed qualified by the pervading sense of muteness. The thimbles of a foxglove standing on the road margin lacked their normal certainty of purple.

(10)

Not caring, not caring, not caring.

Not caring. Muscular demands; someone shouting for rhythm, as in a barroom someone yelling for a special kind of dance music made not for the feet alone but for the whole body. Or was it an old boatman seeking the rhythm of the waves on a day of sunlight and the blue sky over all? Or was it an old rider remembering the gallop of a flighty filly he had mounted in his long-ago youth?

The smell of old goat faint to the right nostril, but almost faded after summer, winter, spring, not now everywhere as bitter as when dropped. She and Martin would have had a goat but that it was a long and twisty road to the North and they couldn't be bothered dragging a goat after them. But after this . . .

After what? After the tiredness, after the burden moving out and down . . . the demand again again, O God . . . not again. But the elastic is not answering, not old at all but weakened and unable to answer the demand that a load be forced down, a crouched load be forced down. . . .

A lattice of light on the floor and the hay wisps below the smoking fuss of my while-ago shoes, the pulled lattice of light and the drawn-out diamonds of sunlight on the floor.

Not caring, not caring, not caring, oh no, not caring, hooves noising in the head all through, the taste of peaches in the mouth and the cool snow and his young shoe above the blue bird.

A lull now, but she knew that he, she, or it was waiting, gathering its strength, its head somewhere amid the seeds in the matted floor of dust—pressed felt it was like, the floor. Perhaps relief was about to pour down from the tattered basket hung on the wall, hissing like water from a sieve as it was released, or perhaps it would sneak out from the spokes of the rusted bicycle wheel that also hung on the wall, wall, wall.

And here it comes again with its angry demands and with the now new head seesawing somewhere and my stomach (where was the room for everything?) heaving over so that one knew the dribble like the . . . the web above, falling from the mouth corner as so often I have seen webs blowing from grasstops in the early early early . . .

Always I pretended to like the sea but I never did. The way I made scissors of my legs and cut his body in two by the pier in the island as I nearly drowned. I can feel the prickle of salt water still on my back. If it could only come. Babby-sweet are you there? In life or out of life? Babby-sweet where are you? Halfway in or out of life? Babby-bitter, babby-bitter, you gather your forces again. This time I promise to help you. Are you there, o part of me, of him, of mankind, you with the eyes of a fisherboy, of the girl with the ball whom I jealoused . . . you are a lovely bold boy. . . . We who roam, we too feel sharply as England's queen. If I were a fish or you were a fish you would slide easily out of me.

The light-diamonds on the floor, faster and faster and each time faster, o tired o my body. High the crane swings, and there is no one in the high cabin; the peeled rods of the basket and the bicycle wheel are high on the wall above me, while here on the sweating floor my nostrils are opening and closing and it's like the bed of honour, the same struggling, the same jee-ee-ee-sus forgive me if I . . . jee . . . oh . . . jee . . . ee take me and break me, fall away babb . . . your shoulders, your shoulders, do not rip the peach skin that is my body, my fish, my kind bloody unborn child, leave me, leave me! I cannot care for you now not even if you were dandled in diamonds. I cannot care for you now if you were all and all and all and all . . . for now the black knot in the kerchief tightens about me . . .

Light now and a creaking door. Bear-woman, bear-woman above me, above us, bear-something-woman, bear-Poll-Poll-woman, your face, your hands above me, your daubed battered face above me. Your terrible hands are not now so rough as I had expected they would be. Easy Poll-bear-woman I cannot, I cannot, I cannot . . .

You tear me! tear me! Here the waves cannot crest, the gulls are all gone and I am being ploughed in love, in birth, in . . . in the other. I smell you Poll-Poll. I smell the piss from your rags, the sweat from your armpits, the smoke from your pipe, but suddenly you are precious you hag you bag. O immortal hand of God, if this comes over me again I shall leave this load behind at what and what and what and what . . . the far gull faded, the wheel hissing in the sun, the clock ticking ever onwards, the crop

241

crashing to the bedroom floor, the blue moth I saw as my eyes rolled like this once once once . . .

The nun taught me how to pray. Not caring not caring not caring. How does prayer begin and to what end and to whom and why? Dickybird smelled too and the soft fur of the tennis ball smelled in my nostril and the puked seawater on the slip smelled as did the broken heather and the spread hay. All had their separate smells. I see the blue moth again and again as then my eyes close my eyes close my eyes close.

My body will not reply to me and it is true that I lie wrongly on my side. I should push, push, c'mon girl, push, and you may win, for this is the Spike, the lucky lovely Spike and the bear-woman is on her knees and the light falls across me and the Poll-bear-woman's face is in the sunsmoke and something immense hangs and I am able and not able and she, her face is sad-cruel above me and she is speaking and I cannot answer so let me go to my ma-a-aan . . . to him I have chosen and whose delight it is to be a wonderful animal to me. So let me free of this, let me cancel this, and I try to think that his head and shoulders and the light is in my right eye corner and the eggshell of my head is a glugger and air is not at the quenching of light of light of l . . . i . . . i . . . i . . . ight . . .

(11)

From the shed came a drawn-out scream. Pipingly, the cry of a newly born infant was heard.

The tinkers cheered and began to punch one another. The girls caught hands and danced extravagantly. Martin's body eased down. Winifred, who had moved uproad, looked back over her shoulder.

The tinkers jeered at her: "Yehoo!"

"Dawloon be praised!" Mickle said. He held his hat over his head. Dickybird's eyes were fast on the shed door.

"You're a father, Claffey!" an old woman shouted.

"I knew he had it in him," another said, amid laughter.

Martin's legs stiffened. His face cracked into a smile. With his thumbnail he made to flick his hatbrim upwards. Recalling that he was bareheaded, he thrust his hands deep into his fob pockets instead. He strutted a few steps.

A boy ran up; he had a birdcage in his hand. "If he's a boy," he said, "here's a linnet for him."

A girl of sixteen groped in her hair. "A comb, if she's a girl," she said. The brilliants of the comb flashed.

"A cat!" cried a dirty-faced boy, who had been groping in a sack he had hitherto carried over his shoulder.

He held the cream-coloured Siamese cat awkwardly—its four legs were drooping. The boy stopped at the gateway and drew the cat's head close to his cheek.

The cry of the infant came stronger than before.

The shed door creaked open and Poll-Poll appeared. She carried an infant wrapped in rags. The younger tinkers pressed forward; the older women, reading Poll-Poll's face, hung back. The lame tinker girl hobbled forward and, snatching the bundle of rags from Poll-Poll's hands, pressed it to her. She then limped towards the wall.

Poll-Poll passed Martin by and came unsteadily to the middle of the area. She looked at her smeared hands. "My hands!" she said, in a barely audible tone of voice. "Look at my hands that lost his wife!"

Martin walked to the gate. Gripping the bars, he raised

himself to tiptoe and pressed the lower part of his body against the iron.

"I lost her!" Poll-Poll moaned. "She quenched on me like a candle's flame. I whispered 'Jesus' in her ear; then she went out the gap of life. With my two hands I killed her. Because I thought I knew the world . . ."

Martin moved still closer to the gate.

"Forgive me!" Poll-Poll went on. "I'm coarse an' ignorant an' old." Raising her voice: "Say somethin', let ye! Breda Claffey's as dead as a salmon on the riverbank—that I swear to ye."

The old woman lurched towards the gateway. "Son," she shouted at Martin, "open your jaws! Screech an' act the mad."

She tried vainly to tear the heavy clothes from the upper part of her body. She stood spread-legged. "Kick me in the groin," she screamed, "till I'm as dead as her!"

Martin turned. His arms stiffened. He began to flex himself on the balls of his feet. He kept one eye corner on the shed. "She isn't dead," he said. "I wouldn't believe it if you swore it on the Cross o' Christ!"

The tinker women pressed upon him. He beat at their hands and heads. As one of the older women fell under a blow, Martin began to leap into the air. Ringed by wailing girls, the women pressed more closely upon him, until by weight of numbers they bore him heavily against the gate. For a time he booted them off.

The women accepted the punishment he gave them and returned to press on him in greater numbers. At last, he swung away from them and, gripping the bars of the gate, began to rock the heavy iron.

He rocked with mounting frenzy until he found the rhythm he sought.

The women, their mouths hanging slack, hung from his back in a tangle of bodies. They adapted themselves to his movements in what seemed an odd ecstasy.

"Breda, you lovely bitch, that I love as man has never loved a woman before," Martin howled. "Come out an' walk with me again. Come out an' swing your arms around my neck. You hear me? You've no complaint o' me. I brought you from the Causeway in the North. We made the bed of honour thirty, forty, seventy times. Come out, I say! For you I raced my cob. Through guns an' bars I brought you to your Honey Spike. Come out, let you . . . The two of us were grand! Only come out, an' then the pony bells will ring for us again. Breda Claffey, listen, I tell you . . ."

Martin's voice had risen to its uttermost. There was foam at his mouth corners.

"The world is thronged with things is lovely at the break o' day!" he shouted. "Come out, you heedless *straip*. Come out, or else I'll drag you by your hair. I tell you that I'll drag you by your shinin', ripplin' hair . . ."

He spread his fingers and slashed them down on his thighs. Recurrently he crouched and drew himself erect. Again he slashed his fingers on his thighs.

"Our Jesus-children are waitin' to be born!" he screamed, and again, "I'll fill your body, till your body's old."

Again gripping the bars, he brought the rocking to a crescendo, until it seemed that the gate must come down. Gradually the movement grew weaker and slower. Dragging his hands convulsively down the iron, Martin fell to his knees at the foot of the gate.

Winifred McQueen came forward. She looked down at Martin, at the women around him and at the bundle of

rags in the arms of the cripple. She looked at the shed
door.

"The light of heaven to her soul," she began quietly.
"Let me say this to ye. I'll take the kid till Puck Fair comes
round again, an' then, when time has done its best, we'll
see what we can do."

She looked around her. Her voice climbed a little as she
said: "Start to cry her, let ye. Go on an' cry her before I
lose my temper with ye. Cry her loud an' keen. A woman's
dead, I tell ye, an' she givin' birth to life. So cry her, you
gang o' paupers from the pit o' hell!"

Clutching the infant, the crippled girl steadied her
crutch beneath her and began to sway and moan. She
ceased as, again, the words came jerking out of Winifred's
mouth.

"An' into your cry put sorrow for all the women who
ever died in such a case. You hear me? Cry her, I tell ye.
Cry her in your milt an' roe. Cry her in your flesh an' bone
an' in your blood flowin' with the moon. Cry her up the
hall of heaven an' to the footstool of the Livin' God. Cry
her till the earth an' sky are wet with travellers' tears."

The tinker women began crying in a low-pitched styl-
ized manner. Gradually the sound grew more abandoned.

The noise was mingled music and lament.

The women dragged their crooked fingers down
through their hair. Some of them, their heads flung back
and their necks taut, tore open their blouses and continued to claw downwards along their throats and breasts.
From mouths open to the full, they bayed and lamented.

The Siamese cat dropped from the boy's arms. For a moment it crouched as if seeking an enemy. The cat then
stretched its trembling legs and began to walk along the
road. It opened its mouth as if to mew, but no sound

emerged. In a patch of sunlight, it stopped for a moment; it looked back at the gateway and again mewed without sound.

The crying ceased.

Listowel-Harvard-Iowa